TEACHER'S

PEST

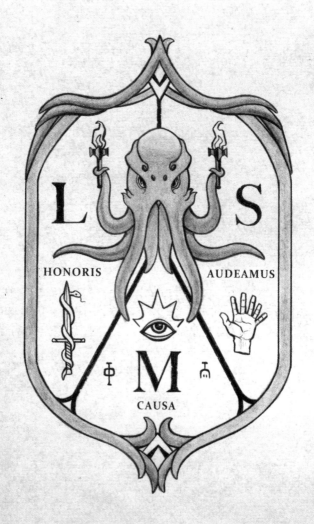

L S

HONORIS   AUDEAMUS

M

CAUSA

TEACHER'S

PEST

TALES FROM

LOVECRAFT
MIDDLE SCHOOL #3

By
CHARLES GILMAN

Illustrations by
EUGENE SMITH

DISCARD

QUIRK BOOKS
PHILADELPHIA

Copyright © 2013 by Quirk Productions, Inc.

Library of Congress Cataloging in Publication Number: 2012935996

ISBN: 978-1-59474-614-7
Printed in China
Typeset in Bembo, House Monster Fonts, and Melior

Designed by Doogie Horner
Illustrations by Eugene Smith
Cover photography by Jonathan Pushnik
Cover model: Griffin Anderson
Production management by John J. McGurk
Lenticular manufactured by National Graphics, Inc.

Quirk Books
215 Church Street
Philadelphia, PA 19106
quirkbooks.com

10 9 8 7 6 5 4 3 2 1

This book
is for
my parents

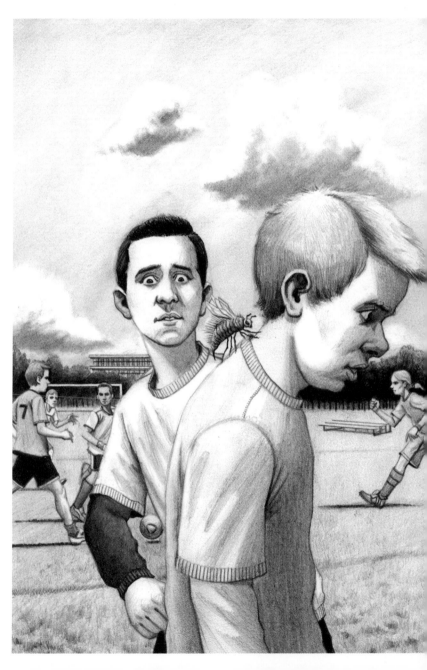

CHAPTER

ONE

"Don't move."

"What's wrong?"

"Something's on your neck."

Glenn Torkells touched the flesh around his throat. "I don't feel anyth—"

"Careful!" Robert Arthur warned. "It's a bug."

"What kind?"

Robert wasn't sure. The creature had two wings, a bright purple abdomen, and a stinger in its tail. "I think it's a wasp."

Glenn froze. Like every other twelve-year-old boy in the world, he understood the first rule of dealing with wasps was to remain absolutely still. If you left them alone, the insects would eventually lose interest and fly away.

Only this one didn't. This one seemed to think the back of Glenn's neck was the perfect place to rest.

The two boys were standing on a soccer field outside Lovecraft Middle School. Glenn was playing goalie; Robert was the defensive fullback. The rest of their gym class was on the far side of the field, watching Lynn Scott launch a penalty kick past Eddie Milano. Coach Glandis tweeted his whistle and shouted, "Hustle! Hustle! Hustle!"

It was a Tuesday morning in early November.

"Is it still there?" Glenn asked.

"Yeah," Robert said.

"What's it doing?"

"Nothing."

"Try pulling it off."

"With my fingers?"

"No, with your toes. What do you think?"

Robert didn't like the idea of touching a wasp with his bare hands. For starters, there was no good place to grab the darn thing. Its head was too small. Its wings were too flimsy. Its purple belly was covered with brittle spikes, like the quills of a porcupine.

"Maybe you *should* move," Robert decided. "Maybe if you spin in circles, it'll get dizzy and fall off."

Glenn stretched out his arms and began twirling like a clumsy ballerina. He spun faster and faster but the wasp didn't budge. From out of nowhere, a soccer ball streaked past him, blasting into the net.

"DEFENSE!" Coach shouted. He came charging down the field, waving his clipboard like a flag to get their attention. "What the heck's going on here?"

Glenn didn't answer; he kept right on spinning.

Coach was dressed in his usual white polo shirt and red track shorts. It was rumored that he wore track shorts every day of the year, even in the winter, even in the worst New England blizzards. "What's wrong with Torkells?" he asked.

"There's a wasp on his neck," Robert explained.

The rest of the class quickly gathered around, pointing and gasping. Everyone agreed it was the biggest wasp any of them had ever seen, that its venom was probably poisonous, or at least extremely painful . . .

"Torkells!" Coach shouted. "Stop spinning and get over here. Let me look at this monster."

Glenn wobbled over, dizzy from all his twirling. Coach peeked inside his shirt collar and the wasp buzzed angrily, warning him to stay back.

"Sheesh!" Coach exclaimed. "Where'd it come from?"

Robert pointed straight up at the sky.

"Can you please get it off me?" Glenn asked.

Coach studied the wasp from different angles. "I'm not sure that's a good idea."

"I don't want to get stung."

"See, that's the problem," Coach explained. "You're *already* stung. It's stinging you right now."

"*What?!*"

The other kids stepped forward for a better look, but Coach ordered them to keep a safe distance. Robert realized the wasp's tail was resting on a round red welt; it was the size of a nickel and growing by the second.

"I could whack him with my clipboard," Coach explained, "but we don't want to break the stinger. We want a nice, clean extraction."

"I'll take my chances," Glenn said. "Just get it off!"

The wasp buzzed again, louder this time.

"All right, on a count of three," Coach said. He raised the clipboard up over his head. "Ready?"

"Yes, yes, just do it!"

"One—"

Glenn grabbed a goalpost, steadying himself, and closed his eyes.

"Two—"

Robert nearly closed his eyes, too. He didn't think he could watch.

"Three!"

CHAPTER

TWO

At that moment—just before Coach brought the clipboard crashing down—the wasp fell from Glenn's neck, dropped to the grass, and died.

"What are you waiting for?" Glenn shouted. He still had his eyes squeezed shut. "Go ahead! Get him!"

"It's over," Robert said.

Glenn opened his eyes and blinked.

Coach reached down and lifted the wasp by a wing. Strangely, all the purple color had drained from its body; it was now just a lifeless gray husk. "Well, I'll be darned. How do you feel, Torkells?"

Glenn pressed his fingers to the welt. "Not so good."

"Better go see the nurse. Robert will take you.

And bring this." He held out the dead wasp, but neither boy wanted to touch it. Exasperated, Coach yanked one of his attendance sheets from his clipboard, wrapped it around the insect, and gave the packet to Robert. "Go on, hurry! This could be serious."

As the boys set out across the field, Glenn tripped over his own feet, and Robert grabbed his shoulder. "Are you all right?"

"I feel weird," Glenn said. "Like I'm all hot."

"Keep walking," Robert said.

The boys entered Lovecraft Middle School through a side entrance. It was a brand-new building, not even three months old, and filled with state-of-the-art technology. The hallways were lined with high-definition video screens; the lockers had electromagnetic doors to prevent theft; there were multiple computers in every classroom. But all these fancy features were masking a sinister secret.

Hidden throughout Lovecraft Middle School were mysterious "gates" that led to an alternate dimension—a sort of world within our world, where a demented physicist named Crawford Tillinghast was planning to overthrow the entire human race. He was raising an army of demons and monsters, disguising them as humans, and sending them into the school. Some looked like teachers; others looked like students. Danger was everywhere, and no one could be trusted.

"What about Miss Mandis?" Glenn whispered. After a few minutes of walking, the boys had finally arrived at the nurse's office, but Glenn stopped just outside the door. "What if she's one of them?"

"We'll know if she tries to bite us," Robert said, and he was only half kidding. "Come on."

It was their first time meeting the nurse. Robert expected to find Miss Mandis dressed in scrubs, like the uniforms worn by nurses in hospitals. Instead, she looked like a regular mom, in a regular blouse and skirt.

She saw Glenn and leapt out of her chair. "What happened?"

Robert handed her the wasp. "This thing stung him. It was purple five minutes ago."

Miss Mandis hurried the boys behind a privacy

screen and told Glenn to lie down on a cot. "Are you allergic to bee stings?"

"I don't think so."

"Have you ever been stung before?"

"Never like this."

"How are you feeling? Headache, nausea, any trouble breathing?"

Glenn scratched the top of his head. "No."

She aimed a lamp at the welt on his neck, then studied it through a magnifying lens. It looked redder now, almost violet, and it had swollen to the size of a marble. "I don't see a stinger anywhere. That's good." She cracked open a cold pack, wrapped it in a washcloth, and pressed it to the welt. "This will stop the swelling. Are you feeling any pain?"

"Only where it got me. It feels like my neck's on fire."

"We'll try some antihistamine." She lifted the cold pack and squeezed some white cream onto the welt. "Let's see if this helps."

Robert was afraid Miss Mandis might tell him to

go back to gym class, so he tried to look busy. He paced around the office, studying all of the health safety posters. After a few moments, he became aware of a faint buzzing noise. He traced it to the nearest window, where three chunky houseflies were throwing themselves at the glass, over and over, desperate to get outdoors.

He reached to open the window but Miss Mandis stopped him. "Leave them be," she said. "I don't want those flies buzzing around my office."

Robert then realized he was mistaken. The flies were *outside* the school and trying to come *in*. They were all flinging themselves against the glass as if they were expecting to smash through.

It might have been funny if it wasn't so weird.

"How are you feeling?" Miss Mandis asked Glenn. "Is the medicine helping?"

He scratched the hair above his neckline. "I'm not sure."

"You should probably go home," she said, reaching for the telephone. "What's your mom's number?"

"She lives in Arizona," Glenn explained.

This was the only thing Robert knew about Glenn's mother: she lived on the other side of the country and hadn't been home in a long time. Glenn never mentioned her, so Robert didn't ask questions.

"How about your father?"

"He's at work."

"Can I call him?"

"His boss doesn't like it. If he gets a phone call, they have to stop the whole line."

Mr. Torkells worked at Dunwich Cosmetics, the last surviving factory within fifty miles. His job was to squirt shampoo into little foil packets that were bound into magazines as free samples. Glenn sometimes bragged that they never had to buy shampoo in a store, because they had thousands of defective shampoo packets stashed in their bathroom.

"This is an emergency," Miss Mandis explained. "What's the phone number of the factory?"

Glenn scratched the top of his head again. "I'm not sure."

"You keep scratching yourself," she observed. "Is your scalp bothering you?"

"That's normal," Glenn said. "It's been itchy all week."

"That's not normal," Miss Mandis said.

She pulled on a pair of latex gloves and redirected the lamp to Glenn's scalp. Then she used a comb to poke through his wavy blond hair. "Oh, dear," she said, sighing.

"What do you see?" Glenn asked.

"A bunch of tiny wingless insects," she explained. "Head lice."

THREE

At the end of the day, after most of the teachers and students had departed for home, Robert walked out to the school parking lot. His friend Karina Ortiz was already there, circling the asphalt and doing ollies on her skateboard. She laughed when she saw Robert coming.

"Oh, no!" she exclaimed.

"Go ahead," he said. "Laugh it up."

It turned out that Glenn Torkells wasn't the only one with head lice. Robert had them, too, and Miss Mandis insisted on treating both boys immediately. She washed their scalps with a medicated shampoo that smelled like tar—and then used electric clippers to

shave off nearly all their hair.

"It's cute," Karina said "You look like a puppy."

Robert studied his reflection in the window of a school bus. "I feel like a skinhead."

"At least you're not a girl. Jill Warrington was growing her hair for seven years, and this afternoon Miss Mandis hacked it all off. Said it was the only way to make sure the bugs didn't come back."

"That seems pretty drastic."

"Apparently they're some kind of super-lice. Very contagious. Twenty-eight cases were reported today. And the usual treatments don't work. You have to go nuclear, or the little grody babies keep hatching."

"Grody?" Robert asked.

Her face flushed. "Sorry. It means gross."

Karina often used slang from the 1980s by accident. Technically, she was only thirteen years old, but she had died three decades earlier in an explosion at Tillinghast Mansion. Thanks to some help from Robert and Glenn, she now roamed Lovecraft Middle School like a regular student—but her spirit was trapped on the school grounds. Which is why she and Robert often found themselves goofing around the parking lot after class.

Today, they were joined by Pip and Squeak, a two-headed rat that had crawled inside Robert's backpack during the first week of school. Robert didn't know where the rats had come from or why they had chosen him to be their master, but after two months of being together, he couldn't imagine life without them. Pip and Squeak were smart, courageous, and (along with Glenn and Karina) his best friends.

"So, where is Glenn?" Karina asked.

"Miss Mandis sent him home early," Robert explained. "He was stung by this crazy purple wasp."

"It's been a really weird week. Today at lunch, a ladybug flew into Emily Sena's mouth. Went right down her throat. And did you hear the janitors are striking?"

"What's that mean?"

"They're not cleaning the school until they get a raise. That's why the trash is piling up. And the bathrooms smell so bad. If you ask me, it's just going to get worse."

Karina pushed off on her skateboard and raced toward the handicapped ramp on the edge of the parking lot. All week long, she had been trying to grind the handrail—to leap three feet off the ground and then slide down the railing while balanced on her skateboard.

Instead, she tumbled onto the pavement, and the board went skidding away from her.

"You know, there's something I don't understand," Robert called. "You can't pick up a pencil. You can't even open a door. So how is it you can ride a skateboard?"

Karina dusted off her jeans and hopped to her feet. "It's complicated. Do you have a lot of homework?"

Whenever Robert asked questions about her life as a ghost, Karina tried to change the subject—but this time, he wouldn't let her. "I want to understand how it works," he said. "Can you ride a bike? Can you paddle a canoe?"

"Just the skateboard," she said. "It was with me when I . . . when the explosion happened." She kicked the skateboard in Robert's direction and he tried to stop it with his sneaker, but the board sailed right through his foot.

"Cool!" he exclaimed. "A ghost skateboard!"

She frowned. "You know I hate that word."

"Right, sorry," Robert said. "What am I supposed to say?"

"You could just stop bringing it up. We could try to have a conversation where you don't call me a ghoulish freak."

"I never said 'ghoulish freak.'"

"What's the difference?"

"Hey, at least you still have your hair," Robert joked.

Karina didn't laugh. "I'd switch places with you any day."

Pip and Squeak made a loud chattering noise. They seemed to be harassing a trail of ants. Robert called for them to leave the bugs alone but the rats kept chattering. They wanted him *to see.*

"All right, all right." He walked over and realized it was no ordinary trail of ants: it was an army. There were hundreds, maybe thousands, marching across the parking lot, ascending the brick wall of Lovecraft Middle School and disappearing through a crack in the mortar. "Look at this," he told Karina. "Where do you think they're going?"

"I'm guessing the cafeteria," she said. "I bet there's plenty of extra protein in tomorrow's lunch menu."

"Maybe this will stop them." Robert removed a bottle of water from his backpack and poured some on the wall, washing away dozens of ants in a miniature tidal wave.

The rest of the army immediately changed course. Now, instead of marching toward the wall, they marched toward Robert. A few of the ants scaled his sneakers, and he kicked them loose.

"They're coming to get me, Karina!" he laughed. "Help!"

The ants spread out in a V-shaped formation, as if they were trying to surround him. Their little legs were remarkably fast, and Robert had to jog backward to stay ahead of them. The ants couldn't catch up, but they didn't stop trying. They chased him all around the parking lot.

Karina watched their activity with growing dismay.

"It's been a really weird week," she said again.

CHAPTER FOUR

Robert lived with his mother in a tiny two-bedroom house at the bottom of a dead-end street. When he arrived home, Mrs. Arthur was waiting at the front door. "Oh, you poor thing," she said, pulling him close. For a moment, he thought she was giving him a hug—but her hands were covered with white latex gloves. She gripped the sides of his head and proceeded to check his scalp, searching for lice that Miss Mandis had overlooked.

"I'm pretty sure she got them all," he said.

"It's the nits you have to worry about," Mrs. Arthur said, raking a spiky comb over the top of his head. "A single louse can lay three hundred eggs in its lifetime."

Robert's mother was a nurse at Dunwich Memorial Hospital. When it came to matters of hygiene, there was no one she trusted more than herself.

"Here's an egg," she said. "And here's another, two more. How could she miss these? Let me pluck them—"

She might have searched Robert's hair for an hour if Pip and Squeak hadn't shifted inside his backpack, rustling the pages of his math notebook.

"What's that?" she asked. "Is something in your bag?"

"Be right back," he exclaimed, twisting out of her reach and hurrying upstairs. Mrs. Arthur was terrified of mice, and she would never allow a two-headed rat to live in her home. So every day Robert smuggled his pets into and out of the house. When he reached his room he unzipped his backpack, and the rats scrambled into a shoe box beneath his bed. "Stay put," he told them. "You nearly got us busted."

When Robert went back downstairs, his mother was placing a bowl of ravioli and meatballs on the kitchen table. "I made Glenn's favorite," she said. "Do you know if he's coming over?"

Robert realized it was already six o'clock, their usual dinner hour. "I guess not," he said.

Glenn had been coming to dinner every night for weeks. He usually ate more food than Robert and his mother combined, but Mrs. Arthur didn't mind the extra cooking. The house felt livelier with a third person around. Glenn was always telling stupid jokes at the dinner table; sometimes he made Robert laugh so hard that milk dribbled out of his nose.

"Well, it'll be nice to have some one-on-one conversation," Mrs. Arthur said. She sat across from Robert and unfolded her dinner napkin in her lap. "How are you liking seventh grade?"

Robert never knew how to answer that question. He couldn't bring himself to reveal the awful things he had learned about Lovecraft Middle School. Mrs. Arthur didn't know anything about Crawford Tillinghast or the secret gates leading to his mansion. Robert hadn't told anyone that Tillinghast was abducting students and teachers, placing their souls in urns, and then using their flesh and hair as disguises for his army of bizarre beasts. How could he expect anyone—even his own mother—to believe him?

"Seventh grade is awesome," Robert said finally.

His mother smiled. "That's so nice to hear."

When they had finished eating, she scooped some ravioli into a plastic container. "Why don't you take these leftovers to Glenn's house?" she suggested. "I bet he'd love it if you stopped by."

Robert wasn't so sure. He'd been friends with Glenn for three months but had yet to see the inside of his house. From the outside, it looked dark and run-down, and Robert was in no hurry to visit.

But Mrs. Arthur was insistent. She pushed the container into Robert's hands. "Go," she said, "before it gets too late."

So Robert put on a coat and hat, went out the front door, and stood underneath his bedroom window. He whistled twice, and, a moment later, Pip and Squeak came scurrying down the drainpipe.

"Follow me, guys," he said. "We're taking a stroll."

The nicest houses in Dunwich, Massachusetts, were built on tall cliffs overlooking the ocean. Robert and Glenn lived two miles away from the coast, in what people still called the "industrial section," even though most of the industries had vanished years ago. The street lamps on his block were all dying or dead, and with just a sliver of moon in the sky, the night seemed especially dark.

Pip and Squeak trotted along beside Robert, occasionally darting at shadows and strange noises, their fangs bared. "Take it easy," he whispered. "Everything's cool."

Glenn lived six blocks away on Liberty Street. His house was a small squat box with dirty yellow aluminum siding. The front yard was littered with junk: car tires, cinderblocks, a section of highway guardrail, a rowboat full of muddy rainwater. More than once, strangers driving by had stopped their cars to wander among the debris, thinking they had stumbled upon some kind of yard sale.

Robert was relieved to see the driveway was empty—this meant Mr. Torkells wasn't home. Glenn's father was a tall, stoop-backed man who rarely spoke and never smiled. Robert was terrified of him. If he thought there was a chance Mr. Torkells might be around, he never would have knocked on the door.

Glenn answered almost immediately.

"What are you doing here?" he whispered.

"Special delivery," Robert explained, holding up the container of food. "It's your favorite. Ravioli and meatballs."

Glenn crossed his arms over his chest. "We have food, Robert. We're not poor."

Robert suddenly felt very embarrassed. He hadn't meant to suggest that Glenn was poor. "It—it was my mom's idea," he stammered. "It's your favorite."

"And you shouldn't stop by people's houses without asking," Glenn said. "It's rude."

"Why are you whispering?"

"I'm not whispering," he said. "My throat is sore."

"Are you sick?"

"I'm just busy right now. I'll see you later."

Glenn turned to go back inside, and Robert glimpsed the welt on the back of his neck. It was darker now, almost black, and had swollen to the size of a golf ball.

"Glenn!" Robert exclaimed. "That thing—are you OK?"

"I'm fine," he said.

"Does it hurt?"

"I'm taking care of it. Good night."

"Maybe my mom should look at it—"

But Glenn had already closed the door.

Pip and Squeak scrambled up to Robert's shoulder, chattering like crazy. Even *they* could tell that something was wrong. "I know," Robert agreed. "I don't get it, either."

As they walked home, Robert replayed the conversation in his mind, trying to understand exactly what he'd done wrong. He couldn't make sense of it.

And what was the deal with the back of Glenn's neck?

Robert was nearly home when he remembered he still had the ravioli. He couldn't imagine telling his mother that Glenn had refused it, so he stopped under a flickering street lamp and opened the container. Pip and Squeak came over to sniff the food, then looked up to Robert with their cutest begging faces.

"Go on," he told them. "It's all yours."

CHAPTER FIVE

The next morning, when Robert arrived at Lovecraft Middle School, the hallways were filled with flies: houseflies, fruit flies, gnats, mosquitoes, and some winged critters he'd never seen before. As soon as he brushed one from his arm, another two landed on his ear or neck or forehead. It was like walking through a barn.

Karina was waiting at his locker.

"When did all this happen?" he asked.

She had no idea. "I went to bed and everything was normal. When I woke up, the swarms were everywhere." A fly landed on Robert's nose and he slapped it away. "People are blaming the janitor strike, but I'm not buying it."

"Why not?"

"Flies aren't born overnight. They hatch as maggots—little baby worms. They take a full week to grow into adults."

"First the wasp, then the lice, now this," Robert said. "Something's up."

"Definitely," Karina said. "Where's Glenn?"

Robert didn't know. Every morning, Glenn stopped by Robert's house on his way to school, but today he didn't show up. "I saw him last night, and he was acting strange."

"Weirder and weirder," Karina said. "What's next?"

They were interrupted by four men marching down the hallway. They wore bright yellow hazmat suits that covered their bodies from head to toe. Their faces were concealed by hooded visors.

"Coming through!" the leader called. "Stand aside, please!"

Each man carried a tank of pesticide marked with a skull and crossbones. They were squirting a gloopy brown liquid on the walls and floor.

"Watch out, please! Watch your step!"

One of the exterminators aimed his spray wand at Robert's feet, and he had to jump to avoid being squirted.

"Hey, careful!" Karina shouted.

The exterminators ignored her and continued their march down the hallway.

"Why are they wearing masks?" Robert asked.

Karina studied the poison dripping down the walls. "This stuff must be really toxic."

It didn't smell toxic to Robert. If anything, the scent reminded him of pancakes. But there was no point in taking chances. He opened his backpack and peered inside. Pip and Squeak came to school with him every morning and usually spent the day snoozing in his locker. "You guys are sticking with me," he said. "Just to be safe."

When Robert arrived in homeroom, he discovered that six more of his classmates had freshly shaved heads. His teacher, Miss Lynch, was standing at the chalkboard with a long wooden pointer, highlighting the anatomy of a housefly.

While other homeroom teachers were happy to take attendance and then let students chat among themselves, Miss Lynch believed that every minute of the school day should be devoted to learning. She often read aloud from the newspaper to inform students of the latest current events. This morning, she was sharing "fun facts" about winged insects.

"Flies taste with their feet," she said. "That's why they're always walking over your food. They especially love sweets: cupcakes, cookies, candies, anything with lots of sugar."

Robert walked to his desk at the back of the classroom. Sitting on his chair was a daddy longlegs about the size of his fist. He used his notebook to brush the bug onto the floor and then sat down.

"Of course, flies don't have teeth, so they can't eat solids," Miss Lynch continued. "Instead they *liquefy* their food by vomiting digestive enzymes onto its surface." The whole class groaned—some of the kids had just finished eating breakfast—but Miss Lynch kept on going. "These enzymes act like a powerful acid, melting the food to a liquid state. Then the fly uses a long snout called a proboscis to slurp it all up."

By the end of the explanation, Robert was ready to vomit himself. Fortunately, Miss Lynch was interrupted by a knock on the door.

"Come in," she called.

It was Howard Mergler, president of the student council. He entered the classroom with the aid of forearm crutches. He had been in a car accident three years before, and now he walked with tremendous difficulty.

"I'm sorry to barge in like this," he said. "May I make a quick announcement?"

"Of course." Miss Lynch set her wooden pointer in the chalk tray and sat down. "Go right ahead, Howard."

Teachers loved Howard Mergler. He was often described as a model student: smart, polite, courteous, responsible, considerate. Howard always tucked in his shirts, and today he was wearing a necktie. On weekends, he volunteered at the public library, reading Shakespeare aloud to blind senior citizens. Earlier in the year, Robert had the chance to become student council president, but he stepped aside so that Howard could serve. He figured that Howard was the perfect kid for the job.

There was just one catch: Howard wasn't really a kid.

The real Howard Mergler was being held hostage inside Tillinghast Mansion. Now his hair and skin and even his crutches were being used as a disguise by a giant insect monster, and Robert and Glenn were the only ones who knew.

"Good morning, everyone," Howard began. "I understand many of you are troubled by the arrival of insects in our school. I'm here to assure you that this is quite common. As winter approaches, it's normal for insects to seek shelter."

Normal? None of this was normal, Robert thought. The wasp on Glenn's neck wasn't normal. Stampeding ants in the parking lot weren't normal.

"Since the janitors are on strike, we're forced to tackle this problem ourselves. That's why I've hired local exterminators to treat the school. You may have already seen them patrolling the hallways. The good news is, the bugs should be gone by the end of today."

Miss Lynch gave him a round of applause. "That's wonderful! Thank you, Howard," she said. "Class? Can you please join me in thanking Howard? Everyone?"

A few students joined in the applause. The rest were busy itching their scalps and scratching their necks. Howard took a modest bow before leaving the classroom.

"Now let's continue with our fun facts," Miss Lynch said. "The average housefly weighs remarkably little, just ten milligrams. That's less than a cotton ball." She stood and lifted the wooden pointer from her desk.

It was weird, Robert thought.

Just a few minutes earlier, hadn't he watched her place the pointer *in the chalk tray*?

Miss Lynch shrieked. The pointer had come alive in her hands, flailing its spindly legs and chirping loudly. In fact, it wasn't her pointer at all—it was a

giant walking-stick insect! Miss Lynch let go and the creature scrambled for the exit, collapsing its bony frame until it was low enough to wriggle under the door.

The students were in hysterics. Miss Lynch fumbled open a bottle of hand sanitizer and squirted it all over her fingers. Everyone was laughing like it was the funniest thing they'd ever seen.

Everyone except Robert Arthur.

He knew that giant walking sticks were just the beginning, and that Howard Mergler wasn't going to fix anything. He knew the infestation at Lovecraft Middle School was going to get a lot worse.

CHAPTER

SIX

In gym class, more wasps were swarming on the soccer field, and they were more aggressive than ever. Coach Glandis kept the students indoors, in the gymnasium, and drilled them on formations until the end of the period.

In the middle of language arts class, a flurry of yellow butterflies burst out of a ventilation duct and chased Mr. Loomis all around his desk.

At lunchtime, a minor panic erupted when Patrick Caulfield discovered a pill bug crawling out of his black bean burrito. Pill bugs look an awful lot like black beans, and soon everyone with a burrito was freaking out.

Dozens of meals were tossed uneaten into the trash.

By the end of sixth period, hundreds of flypaper strips were hanging in all the hallways. They looked like greasy yellow party streamers decorated with twitching black polka dots. The students had to duck to avoid running into them.

But Robert's strangest encounter was still to come. As he was walking to Science, his last class of the day, he spotted a familiar figure in the hallway.

"Glenn!" he called.

Robert almost didn't recognize his friend. Most days, Glenn wore the same green army jacket and tattered blue jeans. But today he was decked out in all-new clothes: new pants, new boots, a new hooded sweatshirt. Robert ran to catch up with him.

"I didn't think you were in school today," he said.

Glenn shrugged and kept walking. "I am."

"You feel better?"

"Sure."

"How's the bite?"

"Fine."

"Is everything all right?"

"Yes."

But things were not all right. This was not how their conversations normally went. His best friend was speaking in a flat monotone. He seemed a million miles away.

"Are you coming over for dinner tonight?"

"What?"

"My mom cooks extra for you," Robert explained. "She needs to know if you're coming."

"I'm not coming."

"Why not?"

"I have plans."

"Plans? What plans?" It didn't make any sense. Robert might as well have been talking to a complete stranger. "Did I do something wrong?"

Glenn turned to face him and spoke very clearly: "Dude, don't you get it? I want you to leave me alone."

Back in sixth grade, before the boys were friends, Glenn used to torment Robert all the time. He was always giving him arm burns and noogies and purple herbies. But none of those pranks ever hurt as much as that one simple sentence: *I want you to leave me alone.*

Robert stopped walking and watched Glenn disappear into the crowd. He thought about the crazy wasp and the hideous boil growing on the back of Glenn's neck.

He realized he couldn't see the boil any longer.

It was concealed by the brand-new hooded sweatshirt that had mysteriously become part of Glenn's wardrobe.

CHAPTER
SEVEN

At the end of the day, Robert opened his locker and found a note waiting on the top shelf. *Come to the library immediately*, it read. *We have important business to discuss.*

The note was signed by Ms. Lavinia, the school librarian. She was Crawford Tillinghast's sister, and the only adult in Lovecraft Middle School who knew about his sinister plans.

Robert arrived at the library and found Ms. Lavinia standing on the circulation desk. She was wearing a tool belt and mounting an electric bug zapper to the ceiling. It looked like a large hanging lantern with a glowing blue coil in the center.

"Trouble with flies?" he asked.

"Moths," she explained. "They're eating the cloth on the hardcover books."

"That's not good."

"They're the least of my worries." She climbed down carefully from the desk and then smoothed out her skirt and blouse. Ms. Lavinia was well past sixty years old, but she had the energy and pluck of a much younger woman. "Where are your pets?"

Robert unzipped his backpack and coaxed Pip and Squeak onto her desk. The rats stretched their paws and yawned. Ms. Lavinia opened a dictionary, and a flat greasy insect wiggled out. It had a sickly gray color and two long quivering antennae. Pip and Squeak pounced on it, pinning the bug with their forepaws.

"Silverfish," Ms. Lavinia said. She riffled the pages and another dozen critters slithered out, fleeing in all directions. "They eat cellulose, the wood pulp used to make paper." After chasing the last of the bugs from the dictionary, she lifted one of the pages. It was speckled with holes small and large, like a slice of Swiss cheese. "In another two weeks, this book will be completely destroyed. All these books, my whole library, ruined."

Pip and Squeak sniffed the silverfish and decided it was too disgusting to eat. They lifted their paws, releasing it, and the insect darted away.

"What can I do?" Robert asked.

"Come with me," Ms. Lavinia said.

Robert, Pip, and Squeak followed her to an office at the back of the library. The room was small and cramped, with stacks of books piled up to the ceiling. The walls were lined with AV equipment: video cameras, digital projectors, laptop computers, and dozens of power strips and extension cords. Karina was already there. She spent most of her day hanging around the library, where the teachers wouldn't notice her.

"Something big is happening," Ms. Lavinia said. She sat on a chair and addressed the children in a low voice. "The lice, the moths, the silverfish—they're all part of it. They're being controlled by a *shaggai*."

"Did you say 'shaggai'?" Robert asked.

"It's the arthropod occupying the body of Howard Mergler."

Robert realized he had glimpsed the shaggai from a distance on the night of the school Halloween dance, when Howard had sprouted two membranous wings and soared into the sky. "What is he, exactly? Some kind of giant bug?"

"More like a giant bug leader," Ms. Lavinia explained. "Imagine a queen bee with power over every bug on earth. Wasps, head lice, walking sticks, silverfish. Howard is summoning all these creatures to Lovecraft Middle School."

"Why?" Karina asked.

"Why, indeed," Ms. Lavinia said. "That's what we need to find out . . ."

Her voice trailed off as she realized they were no longer alone. Standing in the doorway was one of the exterminators. He was dressed in a yellow hazmat suit and his hands clutched a spray wand and a tank of pesticide, as if he were prepared to fumigate the whole office and every living creature inside it.

Pip and Squeak reared up on their hind legs, hissing and baring their fangs. Robert wondered how long he'd been listening, if he'd heard any of Ms. Lavinia's explanation. If maybe he was a shaggai himself.

The exterminator set down his tank and removed his helmet. Robert saw that it was only Ms. Lavinia's husband, Warren.

"Sorry if I frightened you," he said. "I've been doing a little undercover work."

Ms. Lavinia explained that Warren had managed to infiltrate the exterminators by arriving at the school dressed in his own mask and hazmat suit.

"What have you learned?" she asked.

"Nothing good, my dear," he said, sighing. "I'm afraid it's worse than we thought." Warren sank into an empty chair. Pip and Squeak leapt into his lap, nuzzling their faces against his chest, and he scratched both rats behind their ears. "But at least my favorite furry friends are here."

Warren was a marine biologist who worked in a lighthouse down by the waterfront, and he was committed to foiling Tillinghast's plans. He was one of the few adults in town whom Robert trusted completely.

"I'm confused," Robert said. "If Howard is summoning insects *inside* Lovecraft Middle School, why did he hire exterminators?"

"He's just fooling you," Warren explained. "These goofy radiation suits are part of the charade. Watch."

He took an empty coffee mug from his wife's desk and placed the spray wand inside it. Then he pumped the handle on the tank, filling the mug with gloopy brown pesticide. When he finished, Warren raised the mug to his lips.

His wife grabbed his wrist. "Are you crazy? You'll kill yourself!"

"No, I won't. Howard supplied the tanks, and he has no intention of killing anything."

Warren sipped from the mug, grimacing at the taste but forcing himself to swallow. Robert waited for him to choke or gag or clutch his throat, but he seemed perfectly fine.

"It's maple syrup," Warren explained.

Of course, Robert thought. That was the smell he'd recognized that morning—not pancakes, but maple syrup!

"Which is basically sugar," Karina realized. "Instead of killing the bugs, you've been feeding them."

"Exactly," Warren said. "And that's not all."

He explained that real exterminators would set about spraying every inch of an infested space. But Warren's team received instructions to spray only certain hallways. He showed Robert and Karina a floor plan of the school—the targeted areas were highlighted with a yellow marker. It looked like a sunburst, with all the lines converging in the center of the building.

"They're trails," Warren explained. "We spent the day marking trails for the insects to follow."

"Where?" Ms. Lavinia asked. "And why?"

"That's what we need to find out. All the lines lead to one place." He pointed to the middle of the sunburst—a room labeled NURSE'S OFFICE.

"Miss Mandis?" Robert asked. He thought back to the previous morning, when Glenn was lying on her cot. He thought of the three chunky houseflies flinging themselves against her window. "What does she have to do with this?"

"Maybe nothing, maybe everything," Warren said. "I propose we follow the bugs to her office and see what they're doing."

"What if we see a janitor?" Karina asked. One of the strange conditions of her existence was her confinement to the property of Lovecraft Middle School. She lived in the school twenty-four hours a day and spent a good portion of every afternoon hiding from the janitors. She knew all of their schedules and work habits.

"They're still on strike," Ms. Lavinia explained. "At this point in the day, we're probably the only ones left in the school."

That wasn't completely true. It was nearing four o'clock when Ms. Lavinia led them out of the library, and the hallways were empty of students and teachers. But they were far from alone.

Creeping along the edge of the hallway was a long procession of insects—crickets, caterpillars, ants, beetles—all of them following the trails of maple syrup.

"Should we stomp them or something?" Robert asked. "Just to be safe?"

"It won't make a difference," Ms. Lavinia said. "For every one you stomp, a thousand more will be right behind it."

Warren nodded. "They've got us outnumbered."

Even Pip and Squeak seemed intimidated by the sheer number of bugs. Instead of walking beside the critters on the floor, they rode atop Robert's shoulder.

Eventually they arrived at the nurse's office. Along the bottom of the door was a half-inch opening,

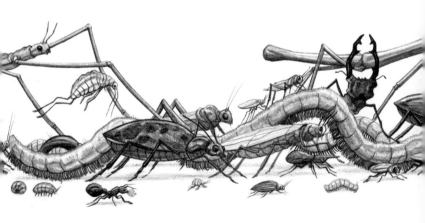

just enough space for the bugs to pass underneath. Ms. Lavinia knocked on the door, waited a moment, and then turned the handle.

The office was empty. The lights were off. The trail of insects passed through the reception area, under the privacy screen, and then disappeared beneath one of the cots.

"Give me a hand," Warren said to Robert.

Together they dragged the cot away from the wall. In the floor was a small slatted vent. The insects were squeezing through the slats and disappearing into a tunnel behind the walls.

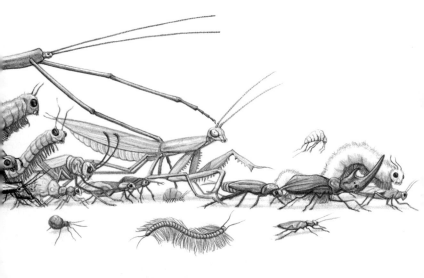

"It's a ventilation duct," Warren explained. "Used for heating and air conditioning. There's a whole network of these ducts traveling all over the school." He knelt down, grabbed a screwdriver from his belt, and used it to remove the vent cover. Then he aimed a flashlight inside. The duct was short and narrow, barely eight inches wide. The long line of bugs marched into the darkness.

"Can you see where they're going?" Karina asked.

"No, not at all," Warren sighed. "And I'm sure this is part of their plan. Now they can travel anywhere in the building, and we're too big to follow them."

"Well," Ms. Lavinia said, "we're not *all* too big."

She turned to the rats who were perched on Robert's shoulder.

CHAPTER
EIGHT

"No way," Robert said.

"Why not?" Ms. Lavinia asked.

"I'm not sending my pets behind those walls. Anything could be back there."

"Exactly. We need to know what's happening."

"And how do you expect them to tell us?"

"Ah," Ms. Lavinia smiled. "That's the fun part."

They returned to her office in the library. Ms. Lavinia approached her shelves of audiovisual equipment and pulled down several boxes of supplies: webcams, flashlights, wire, pliers, Velcro, glue. She spent the next fifteen minutes at her desk, stitching parts onto an old leather glove. Finally she called for the rats to join her.

"All right, boys, step up."

Pip and Squeak hopped onto her desk. Ms. Lavinia fitted a tiny webcam on top of Pip's head, fastening a tiny strap of Velcro under his neck so that he wore it like a helmet. "A perfect fit!" she exclaimed. "By connecting this camera to a laptop computer, we can see everything Pip sees. A rat's-eye view of the ventilation ducts."

"What about light?" Karina asked.

"That's where Squeak comes in." She fitted a second helmet on top of Squeak. This one was equipped with a small but very bright LED bulb. "He'll illuminate the vent so we can see."

The helmets were secured by the split leather glove that the rats wore like a jacket. They seemed amused by the outfit, as if they were dressing up like characters in a play. Pip opened his mouth in a hideous snarl while Squeak aimed the headlamp at his twin, casting terrifying shadows on the wall.

"You see?" Ms. Lavinia said. "They love it."

The group returned to the nurse's office with the

laptop computer and a hundred-foot-long yellow cable. "This wire transmits the camera imagery to the computer," Ms. Lavinia explained.

"What if we run out of wire?"

"We'll give it three sharp tugs. That will be their signal to turn around and come back. Until then, they just need to follow the bugs as far as they can."

Robert knelt down and explained these instructions to Pip and Squeak. It was the strangest thing: he had found he could give the most complicated directions to his pets, and they always understood exactly what he wanted. He assumed it was because they had two brains, that they were twice as smart as an ordinary rat. Sometimes Robert had only to *think* what he wanted, and his rats would obey the order.

But this afternoon, he needed to be a little more persuasive. Pip and Squeak glanced into the duct and shook their heads. *Maybe you should crawl in first*, they seemed to be suggesting.

"You're the only ones who can fit," Robert said. "If there's any trouble, I'll grab the wire and reel you in." He pulled on the cable to demonstrate, raising them off the floor. Pip and Squeak flailed their legs until he set them down again. They were not amused.

Warren powered up the laptop and started the camera program. A grainy image of Robert's face appeared on the computer screen. This was because Pip and Squeak were looking at him, and the camera was transmitting everything the rats could see.

"Perfect," Warren said. "All systems go."

"All systems except Pip and Squeak," Karina observed. She had spent enough time with the rats to know their moods. "They still look scared."

Don't be scared, Robert thought. *I'll be watching the whole time. I won't let anything bad happen.*

He knew Pip and Squeak could hear his thoughts and he knew they trusted him. He had always been a loyal parent to them; he changed their litter once a week, he sneaked them vegetables from the dinner table, he let them sleep under his blankets on cold nights. If Robert said the ducts were safe, then Pip and Squeak believed they were safe.

His rats approached the trail of insects, hissing loudly, and bugs scattered out of the way. Pip and Squeak cut in front of a stinkbug, then looked over at Robert and seemed to grin.

"They're doing it!" Warren said. "You convinced them!"

Karina looked at Robert. "What did you say to them?"

He shrugged. "They just needed a pep talk, that's all."

The rats followed a black beetle into the duct and soon they were swallowed up by the darkness. Everyone turned to look at the shaky image on the laptop computer. The rats were still following along behind the black beetle—only now, seen in extreme close-up, it looked like a lumbering rhinoceros. As Pip and Squeak crept along, Robert fed out more wire; Warren was measuring every handful. "That's about fifteen feet."

Ms. Lavinia consulted a map of the school. "They're moving east. Toward the swimming pool."

The helmets were working perfectly; the flashlight illuminated the entire duct. From the rats' perspective, it appeared to be a large, boxy tunnel with brushed aluminum walls.

"Twenty feet," Warren counted. "Twenty-five."

As they watched, Robert began to relax. Pip and Squeak were doing fine. The duct seemed safe and well lit. Maybe the task wasn't so dangerous after all.

Eventually, the rats arrived at an intersection. The passage divided into three ducts, one of which was much larger than the others. The bugs were moving into this new, larger passage, but Pip and Squeak hesitated.

"Go on," Warren whispered. "Follow the bugs."

Yes, Robert thought. *Follow the bugs.*

Pip and Squeak stepped forward, turning left and climbing into the new duct. This one was three times the size of the original duct—large enough for a person to squeeze through. It seemed to be sloping downward.

"Fifty feet," Warren counted.

"Where are they going?" Robert asked.

"Downstairs," Ms. Lavinia said.

"There's a downstairs?" Robert's copy of the student handbook included a floor plan of Lovecraft Middle School, but it didn't mention anything about a basement.

"It's off-limits to students," Karina explained. "There's a mechanical room with boilers and air vents. The drains for the swimming pool. All the machines that keep the school running."

"Seventy-five feet," Warren said.

"Maybe we should call them back," Robert said. "I didn't know there was a downstairs."

"Just another minute," Ms. Lavinia said. "Let's see how far they can go."

The rats traveled a full ninety feet before stopping. They appeared to have reached the edge of a chasm. The duct continued on the other side of a three-foot gap. Pip and Squeak peered down into the void, but their headlamp revealed nothing except a yawning black pit. It seemed bottomless.

"End of the road," Robert said. "Time to turn around."

Pip and Squeak were looking across the chasm. The duct continued on the other side, and the bugs were having no trouble getting across; they simply climbed over via the walls and kept going. Pip and Squeak stared after them, anxiously pacing from side to side.

"They see something," Warren said. "Is there any way to make the camera zoom in?"

Ms. Lavinia laughed. "I built streaming-video camera helmets for a two-headed rat in fifteen minutes, and you're complaining that they don't have a zoom lens?"

Pip and Squeak stepped closer to the edge of the

gap, as if they were contemplating a jump.

"Forget it, guys," Robert called into the duct. From their rat's-eye perspective, it looked like a leap across the Grand Canyon. "You'll never make it."

"It's too bad," Warren said. "They're so close."

Robert tugged three times on the wire, the signal for the rats to stop and turn around. But they ignored his call. They seemed to be calculating the size of the gap.

I'm serious, he thought. *Come back right now. I know you can hear me.* Pip and Squeak backtracked several steps, and Robert relaxed. *Thank you.*

Then the rats sprinted forward, a running start.

"No!" Robert shouted.

Pip and Squeak hit the edge of the chasm and launched themselves across the opening. For a moment, the camera feed was a blur. Robert was so nervous, he forgot to breathe.

Then the image slammed into focus.

For a split second, he saw two claws gripping the edge of a metal precipice, desperately trying to lift themselves to safety.

Then the image was all blurry again.

Before Robert could even think, the camera wire whipped through his fingers, popped out of the computer, and disappeared through the vent.

The screen went dark.

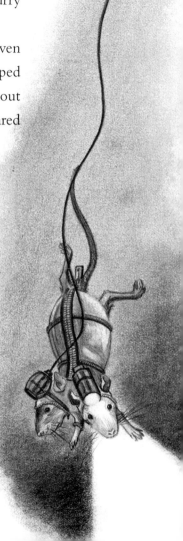

CHAPTER
NINE

If Robert thought he had any chance of fitting into the duct, he would have leapt right through the vent.

"This is going to be fine," Warren insisted. "We'll just go down to the basement and get them out."

"Where's the basement?" Robert asked.

Ms. Lavinia led them down the hallway to a door labeled MECHANICAL ROOM: AUTHORIZED PERSONNEL ONLY. Robert tried the door but it was locked.

"The janitors have the key," Karina said.

"The janitors are on strike," Robert said. He threw his weight against the door, hitting it with his shoulder, like he'd seen action heroes do in the movies. Of course, that did nothing except hurt his shoulder. Warren grabbed his arm, trying to settle him down.

"Take it easy," he said. "You can't get through that way."

Robert turned to Karina. "What about you?"

"Me?"

"Can't you just squeeze through a keyhole or something? Turn yourself into mist and roll under the door? What kind of ghost are you?"

Karina's lower lip trembled, as though she was going to start crying. She turned abruptly and ran off down the hall. Robert threw up his hands in frustration. What was wrong with her? *He* was the one who had lost his pets. Not her. He felt like *he* was going to start crying.

"Calm down," Ms. Lavinia said.

"You made me do this!" he shouted. "You promised they would be OK!"

"They *will* be OK," she insisted. "I'll find a way to unlock this door, but it's not going to happen immediately." At night, Ms. Lavinia was a prisoner inside

Tillinghast Mansion, and she waited on her brother like a servant. "I'm sure Crawford has a set of keys. I'll spend all night looking for them."

"And what am I supposed to do? Just leave Pip and Squeak in the air duct?"

"They're rats. They can survive a night in an air duct. Some rats live their whole lives in air ducts. They're tough animals."

"You don't know them like I do," Robert said.

It was true that Pip and Squeak could be brave when they needed to be. Once, when a giant boa constrictor had sneaked through Robert's bedroom window, they had rushed to his defense. But just because his pets were brave didn't mean they weren't scared. Pip and Squeak had fears just like everyone else—and now they were trapped behind the walls of Lovecraft Middle School.

"We'll take care of this tomorrow, I promise," Ms. Lavinia said. "Now go home and try not to worry about it."

That was going to be impossible. Robert didn't see

how he would eat, sleep, or do anything until he had them back. He left the school in a daze. While crossing the street, he stepped in front of an on-coming pick-up truck. The driver swerved, missing him by inches, then blasted his horn.

When Robert arrived at his house, his mother could tell he was upset. "Your hair looks like it's growing back already," she said, running her fingers through his buzz cut. "Were the other kids teasing you?"

"No," Robert said. In fact, he'd forgotten about the buzz cut altogether. Who could worry about hair at a time like this?

"At work they're calling it a head lice epidemic. They're saying half the school is infected. Is that true?"

"More than half," Robert said. By the end of the day, he felt like most of his classmates had their heads shaved.

"Maybe you should stay home tomorrow," Mrs. Arthur said. "Maybe you should avoid the school until they get everything straightened out."

"No," Robert insisted. "I need to go back." As far

as he was concerned, tomorrow couldn't come soon enough.

Dinner was quiet that evening. Robert didn't feel like talking, so his mother didn't ask lots of questions. Once again she filled a container with leftovers. "Since Glenn enjoyed my ravioli so much, why don't you run this over to his house?"

This time Robert didn't hesitate. He was desperate to talk to Glenn, to tell him that Pip and Squeak were in trouble. If that news didn't jolt his friend back to normal, nothing would.

He walked the same route as the night before, but the trip seemed twice as long without his pets to keep him company. It also seemed twice as cold. Robert shoved his hands in his pockets, wishing he'd worn a heavier jacket. He stepped over a pothole full of water, knowing it would probably freeze before morning.

When he arrived at Glenn's house, he noticed a few things were different. For one thing, the old rowboat on the front lawn was gone. The cinder blocks were stacked in a neat pile at the end of the driveway.

And the rest of the junk had been moved to the curb for trash pickup.

The driveway was still empty, so Robert knew Mr. Torkells wasn't around. He climbed the porch steps and rapped his knuckles on the screen door.

There was no answer.

"Glenn!" he called, knocking louder.

Finally, the door was opened by a woman cradling a baby. "I thought I heard someone," she said, smiling. "Lizzie and I were upstairs when you knocked."

The baby was wrapped in a pink blanket; she kicked her tiny legs and squealed. The woman rocked from side to side until the infant stopped crying. Then she patted her on the back and cooed into her ear.

"Um, is Glenn home?" Robert asked.

"You just missed him," she said. "Are you Robert?"

"Yeah."

The woman extended her free her hand. "I'm Beth. Glenn's mom. He's told me a lot about you."

Robert shook her hand. "You live here?"

"I've been away for a while. Lizzie and I came

home yesterday."

"Oh," Robert said. He was too surprised to say anything else. He had never imagined that Glenn's mother would be so . . . normal.

She held open the door, inviting Robert inside. "Would you like to join us for dinner? Glenn and his

dad went out to get a pizza."

"I already ate," Robert said.

"You could join us anyway," she said. "I've got root beer. And I bet Glenn would be happy to see you."

Robert wasn't so sure about that. He suddenly understood why Glenn was acting so strange, and the answer had nothing to do with the purple wasp or the welt on the back of his neck.

"I should probably go," he said.

"I'll tell Glenn you stopped by. Did you want to leave a message?"

"Yeah," Robert said. "Can you tell him—"

But he couldn't finish the rest of the sentence. What had happened to Pip and Squeak was so awful, he couldn't bring himself to say it out loud.

"Tell him I'll see him in school tomorrow."

CHAPTER
TEN

The next morning, Robert woke in darkness. A layer of frost coated his bedroom window, blocking out the sunlight. On the radio, the DJ announced that the temperature was a chilly twenty-nine degrees.

Robert dressed and went downstairs. Mrs. Arthur left early for work every morning, so he was used to making his own breakfast. Out of habit, he grabbed three cereal bowls from the cabinet. He was usually joined at the kitchen table by Pip and Squeak, and his pets insisted on different cereals (Pip preferred regular Cheerios; Squeak liked the honey nut flavor). Upon realizing his mistake, Robert returned all three bowls to the cupboard. He was too nervous to eat breakfast anyway.

He was putting on his coat when he discovered a note by his mother, tucked inside one of the pockets: "Remember, hair grows back! Cheer up and have a great day!" It was wrapped around a special treat: a Hershey's chocolate bar with almonds. Robert nearly left the candy at home—he couldn't imagine regaining his appetite anytime soon—but decided to leave it in his pocket, just in case.

When he arrived at Lovecraft Middle School later that morning, all the insects were gone. No swarms were buzzing in the hallway, no beetles or crickets were marching across the floor. The strips of flypaper had been removed and discarded. If it weren't for the heads of his classmates—by now, nearly everyone in school was sporting a buzz cut— Robert might have wondered if the past few days had just been a bizarre dream.

He went straight to the library. Ms. Lavinia was standing on the circulation desk and removing the bug zapper from the ceiling. She saw him coming and frowned.

"Did you get the key?" Robert asked.

"Not yet."

"But you promised—"

"I'm sorry, Robert. My brother has a set in his study, but he was up working all night. I'll have to try again this evening."

Robert realized that meant waiting another twenty-four hours before taking action. A whole extra day of imagining the worst. He couldn't stand it.

"Never mind," he said. "I'll find the key myself."

Ms. Lavinia hurried down from her desk and followed Robert out of the library. The hallway was crowded with students opening their lockers and removing their coats. She looked like she wanted to yell, but the crowds forced her to speak in a whisper. "What are you planning?"

"I'll cross over," Robert said. "I've done it before. I can do it again."

Most of the gates to Tillinghast Mansion were well hidden, but recently Robert had discovered one at the bottom of the school swimming pool. He knew that if he swam through it, he would emerge in a small pond located on the side of the house.

"You'll never make it to the study," Ms. Lavinia said. "You'll be lucky if you get through the front door." Still whispering, she reminded Robert that the mansion was home to lots of demons and monsters, all of them desperate for a human "vessel" that would allow them to enter the school unnoticed.

"I have to try," Robert insisted. "I can't just sit here and do nothing. Pip and Squeak need my help."

Ms. Lavinia seemed to understand there would be no talking him out of it. She took Robert by the elbow and led him in a different direction. "If you're going to insist on crossing over, at least let me show you a shortcut."

Just then the eight-twenty bell rang, signaling the start of the school day, and students began filing into their homerooms. Ms. Lavinia led Robert to the backstage entrance of the school auditorium. The wings of the stage were a dark and shadowy space, cluttered with clarinets and cellos, tubas and timpani drums, along with dozens of music stands and folding chairs.

Ms. Lavinia directed Robert's attention to a navy blue drape at the rear of the stage. "You need to walk behind that curtain. When you reach the ladder, start climbing. Be as quiet as you can. Sound can travel through a gate, and if you're too loud, my brother will hear you coming."

"How do I get the key?"

"I wish I knew. I've heard him say the keys are in the lock, but I don't know what that means."

"The keys are in the lock?" Robert asked. "That doesn't make sense."

"My brother doesn't make a lot of sense. You'll just have to search his entire study. Be careful."

As Robert ducked behind the curtain, his stomach did little flip-flops. This was his first time venturing into Tillinghast Mansion alone, and he wished that Glenn or Karina were going with him.

Fortunately, the ladder was easy to find—it was a series of metal rungs mounted to the cinder-block wall. Robert planted his feet on the lowest one and climbed hand over hand. He was ten feet above the stage when he recognized the familiar swampy stench of the mansion; it was too dark to see the gate, but he could feel its energy, drawing him higher and making the climbing easier. He had nearly reached the top of the ladder when all of the rungs abruptly disappeared, and he realized he was standing on solid ground.

And he was no longer alone.

"What are *you* doing here?"

CHAPTER
ELEVEN

"I told you I didn't want to be disturbed."

The voice came from the other side of the curtain. It was dry and rasping—not just old but ancient. Robert's hands began to tremble, as if his subconscious sensed a threat of grave and immediate danger.

"Forgive me, Your Excellency. I'm sorry to barge in like this." Robert recognized this second voice as Howard Mergler's. "I have good news, and I wanted to share it right away."

Robert shifted the curtain a fraction of an inch, just enough to peer into the room. He saw an enormous study. The walls were lined with tall shelves of old, cloth-covered books. Howard sat in a guest chair, a clipboard of notes balanced on his lap. Robert couldn't see the man sitting across from him, yet he knew at once that it must be Crawford Tillinghast.

"First frost arrived this morning," Howard continued, "but thanks to some smart planning, I managed to stay ahead of it. I've now corralled more than a hundred thousand insects."

"Where are you keeping them?"

"In an underground burrow. Directly below the soccer field. With enough heat and food to ensure that reproduction continues throughout the winter. By springtime, the army will be ten times its current size!"

If Tillinghast was pleased, he didn't show it. "What if someone discovers them?"

"Impossible, Your Excellency. The entrance is in the basement mechanical room. No teachers or students are allowed down there."

"Suppose someone trespasses."

"It's very well concealed. Not even the janitors will discover it."

Robert's stomach growled and he realized that

skipping breakfast had been a terrible mistake. Now his appetite was catching up with him, and the timing couldn't be worse. He clutched his hands over his belly, but it squealed again.

"Did you hear that?" Tillinghast asked.

"Hear what?"

"That noise. Like the howl of a dog."

They both waited for the sound to be repeated, and Robert was relieved to find that his stomach had settled down.

"Probably just my sister snooping about," Tillinghast concluded. "All last night, I could hear her pacing outside my office. Back and forth, back and forth, waiting for me to leave. She's up to something, I'm afraid."

"I'll interrogate her at once," Howard offered.

"Another time. I want to see this burrow you've created."

Howard was surprised. "But is it safe to leave the study? If Your Excellency has concerns about a security breach . . ."

"It will be fine for a few minutes. Ethugu will keep an eye on things."

Tillinghast rose from his chair and Robert ducked behind the curtain. The old man's voice was awful enough; Robert was too afraid to actually look at him. His hands were still shaking beyond his control.

He waited until Tillinghast and Howard had left the study, then lingered in his hiding place for another minute, listening for sounds or movement. There were none. He peered out from behind the curtain, scanning the study from one end to another.

Ethugu will keep an eye on things.

What was Ethugu? Where was Ethugu? Robert had no idea. He seemed to have the room entirely to himself. He imagined that someone (or, more likely, some *thing*) named Ethugu was standing guard just outside the door. He would have to be very quiet.

But now what?

The keys are in the lock. Robert stepped into the study, and the wooden floorboards creaked beneath his feet. Over the door was a wide tapestry portraying a group of men and women dressed in bright red tunics, like ancient Romans; they were holding hands in a circle, surrounding a ring of fire. As Robert studied the tapestry, he felt like he was being watched—but when he glanced over his shoulder, he saw that he was still alone.

He began pacing around the room, pulling on desk drawers and cabinet doors, but everything in the study was locked and none of the locks contained keys. In one corner stood a large wooden globe; Robert spun it with his fingers, checking for Africa or Australia or any of the places he was learning about in Social Studies. He realized that none of the continents on this globe looked even remotely familiar. It was a map of some other place, a world whose oceans were teeming with serpents and whales and leviathans.

Robert knew he was running out of time. He turned to the bookshelves, as if one of the thousands of dusty hardcover volumes might contain the answer. Many of the books were so old that their titles were illegible, but they appeared to be arranged alphabetically by author. Jonathan Byrd. Alfred Cable. Eugene Carp.

The keys are in the lock.

Suddenly, Robert had an idea. He circled the perimeter of the study, following the author surnames, moving from C and D to K to L, from La and Le to Li and Lo.

Until he found the lock.

The Collected Works of John Locke.

As soon as Robert lifted the volume from the shelf, he realized it was no ordinary book. Hundreds of keys spilled from it and clattered to the wooden floor.

Robert ducked behind the desk. He was terrified that Ethugu, hearing the noise, would enter the study to investigate. As he huddled in wait, he realized the book was nothing more than a box; its pages had been hollowed out to form a sort of hiding place.

Unfortunately, it contained more keys than Robert could fit in his pockets. He would have to search until he found the right one. All the keys were different shapes and sizes, but each one was labeled with a tiny inscription: "East Ext. Door" or "Rm. 223" or "Art

Closet." As Robert sifted through them, he again felt the sensation of being watched. It was stronger than ever, but the door to the office remained closed.

"Come on," he whispered to himself, checking the labels as quickly as he could. "Where are you?"

He was answered by a wet gurgling noise, the sound of water swirling down a clogged drain. Robert looked over his shoulder to see a pair of blinking blue eyes looking back at him.

No, *several* pairs of eyes, dozens of them, all embedded in a blob of green ooze descending from the ceiling.

Robert looked up and discovered that he had never been alone in the study. This thing, this eyeslime, this Ethugu—it had been clinging to the ceiling and watching him the entire time.

The creature bulged toward him and Robert backed away, slipping on the keys and losing his balance. He fell to the floor, and Ethugu oozed down all around him, blinking furiously, surrounding him in a cocoon of glistening green mucus. Everywhere

Robert looked, Ethugu looked back at him. Its eyes were furious, as though it was daring him to try to break free.

Instead, Robert remained perfectly still, his arms at his sides. After a few moments, he noticed that the slime seemed to be getting darker, that everything was getting darker.

But it was only a trick of his imagination. In truth, he had depleted all the oxygen in the cocoon. Robert was blacking out.

CHAPTER TWELVE

The next time Robert opened his eyes, Ethugu was gone. So was the study. He found himself sitting on a chair in a windowless room not much bigger than a closet.

Sitting across from him was a giant insect, five feet tall, with the abdomen of a beetle and the head of a giant fly.

Robert leapt up, teetered for a moment, and then fell back into his seat. His ankles were bound to the legs of his chair with several coils of rope.

The shaggai waved its limbs, gesturing for Robert to remain still. Its mandibles clacked open and shut, producing a loud *rat-tat-tat* that sounded like an old-fashioned typewriter.

Robert strained to untie the ropes, but the knots were just out of reach. He glanced around the room, looking for a knife or something sharp. The walls were lined with shelves, and the shelves were filled with dozens of brass and silver urns. Otherwise the room was empty.

The creature kept clacking its jaws until a figure opened the door. "Good, you're awake," said Howard Mergler. "We can get started."

"What time is it?" Robert asked.

"In your world, it is almost eleven o'clock."

"I've missed three classes. The teachers will notice I'm not there. They're going to come looking for me."

"You'll be back in class soon enough," Howard promised. "The extraction takes only a few minutes." He removed a silver urn from the shelf and used a dark marker to write Robert's name on the side. "The silver ones have more space than the bronze. An extra inch or two may not seem like much, but you'll appreciate it later."

"Later?"

"After you've surrendered your vessel. My brother will wear it so that he can join me in your world. He's the same height as you, so it ought to be a perfect fit. We're both very excited."

The shaggai clapped its forelimbs together; it seemed to be applauding. Robert was less excited. He understood that his spirit, or whatever was left of it, would be going into that urn, where it would be trapped for hundreds, or even thousands, of years.

"You're very lucky," Howard continued. "Master is going to perform the extraction himself. He's anxious to meet you. But before you take your place on the shelf, we must get some information. We need to know why you were snooping in Master's office."

"I wasn't snooping—"

"You were looking for a key. How did you know about the Locke?"

Robert knew that every minute he played dumb would be another minute he spent in his own body. "I don't know what you're talking about."

"Did Master's sister help you?"

"No," Robert said.

"She must have!"

"I swear, she didn't. Ms. Lavinia didn't say anything."

The shaggai twitched its antennae and its jaws produced another clacking noise. It sounded like it was laughing.

"I see," Howard said, smiling. "You don't know what I'm talking about, and yet you know exactly whom I mean when I say 'Master's sister.'"

Robert cringed as he realized his mistake.

"What else has she told you?"

"Nothing."

"She's helping you, isn't she? She and her husband—that so-called scientist. They're trying to thwart Master's plans!"

"I don't know anything," Robert insisted.

The conversation went back and forth for several minutes until Howard finally gave up. "If you won't tell me, you'll definitely tell Master," he sighed. "He's not as patient as I am." And with that he left the room.

Robert found himself alone with the shaggai. How long would he have until Howard returned with Tillinghast? Two minutes? Three?

What could he do with three minutes?

Robert emptied his coat pockets, searching for anything that might help him escape. He had a dollar in change, a pencil, the chocolate bar (now half melted), and his house key. He tried rubbing the key against the rope; it started to fray the outer fibers, and he sawed faster, back and forth. He had seen this trick in an old movie, but he soon realized it wouldn't work in real life. There simply wasn't enough time. After a minute of furious slicing, he had barely made a mark in the rope.

The shaggai again clacked its jaws. Robert glanced up and realized the creature was observing him. "Don't worry," he muttered, "I'm not going anywhere." The shaggai shook its head and then extended one of its six segmented limbs. It seemed to be pointing at something in Robert's lap.

The chocolate bar.

"You want this?" Robert asked.

The shaggai nodded and its antennae twitched wildly, as if the simple promise of chocolate made it giddy with pleasure. *Flies love sweets*, Miss Lynch had told the students. *Anything with lots of sugar.*

Robert had an idea. He peeled off the wrapper and pressed the chocolate bar into the ropes binding his ankles.

"Go ahead," he whispered.

The beast stood up and tottered over, intrigued. It seemed cautious, as if Robert's invitation was somehow too good to be true.

"It's all yours," Robert assured it. "Eat up."

The shaggai knelt on the floor. Its mandibles parted, and a hideous proboscis emerged, like a long glistening black tongue. It sniffed all around Robert's ankles before discovering the chocolate and spraying it with a greasy black oil.

The digestive enzymes immediately melted the candy and kept right on working, dissolving the rope's fibers until Robert was finally able to shake his ankles free. The shaggai didn't even notice. It was still down on the floor, slurping up the liquefied chocolate, seemingly intoxicated with pleasure.

"Thanks," Robert said. "Bon appétit."

Upon opening the door, he found himself in a twisting hallway lined with rooms. He heard footsteps coming from one direction, and so he ran the other way. He had to find a gate, fast.

Among the many weird things about Tillinghast Mansion was that it seemed bigger on the inside than it looked from the outside. The building had more rooms than a small hotel, but the doors were all identical and unnumbered, so there was no way to tell them apart. Hallways coiled around corridors and then abruptly dead-ended, like paths of a labyrinth. Robert began to fear that he was running in circles, passing by the same rooms again and again.

He tried a different direction, turning a corner and running straight into the school nurse, Miss Mandis.

She seemed to have come out of nowhere. Robert struck her so hard that they nearly fell to the floor.

"Robert Arthur?" she asked. "Is that you? Where are we? What is this place?"

"You don't know?" he asked.

She looked frightened and confused. "Five minutes ago, I was in my office. I was getting some cotton balls from the storeroom. I used a stepladder to reach the top shelf, just like I always do, only this time something happened . . ." She looked around in astonishment. "Next thing I know, I'm in this weird hotel."

"You crossed over," Robert explained.

"Crossed over? What do you mean?"

It would take too long to convince her of the truth. "I can explain after we cross back." He spied a door leading to the outside at the end of the hallway. "Right now we need to get out of here."

"But where *is* here?"

"Please," he insisted. "Just follow me, and keep as quiet as you can."

They exited the mansion and descended a creaky wooden staircase to the back lawn. The grass was covered with red, orange, and mustard-colored leaves. Miss Mandis glanced about in awe. "I don't understand," she kept saying. "What happened to Lovecraft Middle School?"

"Please, keep your voice down," Robert said, glancing around anxiously. They were alone for the moment, but surely Howard had discovered his escape by now. In another few minutes, everyone in the mansion would be searching for him.

"Why do I need to keep my voice down? Whose house is this anyway?"

Miss Mandis wouldn't stop talking, so Robert walked faster, leading her to the small pond on the side of the mansion. It was only a few feet across and surrounded by weeds. The surface was covered with a skin of bright green algae.

"All right," Robert said, taking a deep breath. "This is going to sound crazy, but we need to jump in this water."

Miss Mandis laughed. "Very funny, Robert."

"I'm serious. There's a gate at the bottom of this pond. A sort of portal. We need to swim through it to get back to the school." He had used the gate only once before—and nearly drowned in the process—but if it still worked, they would emerge to find themselves in the school's indoor swimming pool.

"You're crazy!" Miss Mandis exclaimed. "I'm not jumping into that filthy water." She pointed to the driveway. "Let's just walk back."

"It doesn't work that way," Robert insisted.

"Better yet, I'll call my sister. She can pick us up."
Miss Mandis whipped out her cell phone and punched
in a number. She was dismayed to find it didn't work.
"That's weird. I can usually get a signal anywhere . . ."

"There's no service here," Robert explained.
"We're not in our world anymore."

Across the lawn, the front door of the house
opened and Howard Mergler stepped outside. Miss
Mandis saw him and exhaled a sigh of relief. "Oh,
thank goodness. I'm sure Howard will know what to
do." She waved to him. "Over here, Howard!"

"We need to jump," Robert insisted.

"Don't be silly. Howard will help us. He's always so
thoughtful and considerate."

Howard walked swiftly in their direction. He
moved so much more quickly without the forearm
crutches. Robert realized he had no time to convince
Miss Mandis; he would have to return to Lovecraft alone.

"I'll come back," he promised. "I'll try to rescue
you before they perform the extraction."

She laughed. "Rescue me? What do you mean?"

"I'm really sorry, Miss Mandis. I have to go."

Robert turned to leap into the pond but she grabbed his arm. Her eyes flickered green and bulged outward, tripling in size. "You're not going anywhere!" she shrieked. "Master has questions for you!"

Two long feelers burst through her forehead and rose twelve inches above her hair. Flesh fell away from her face in dry, flaky strips; she was shedding her vessel the way a snake molts its skin. Robert realized that Miss Mandis had been fooling him all along, speaking loudly so that Howard would hear and come to her aid.

He tried shaking off her grip. When that didn't work, he lunged toward the pond, dragging Miss Mandis with him, and together they toppled into the water. She shrieked and flailed about, unable to swim.

Robert didn't stick around to help. Taking a deep breath, he plunged into the pond, propelling himself deeper and deeper until he felt the unmistakable sensation of crossing over. Then the light in the water changed, and Robert knew it was safe to head for the surface. Swimming in his clothes was difficult, but having done it once before, he knew he could do it again. He kicked his feet and paddled his arms until he crested the surface.

As expected, he had arrived in Lovecraft Middle School's natatorium—an indoor Olympic-size swimming pool with ten lanes, three diving platforms, and bleachers to hold a crowd of hundreds.

What he did not expect to see was his old friend Glenn Torkells, sitting in the front row of the bleachers and munching on a bag of gummy worms.

"Now *that* was a real dumb move," Glenn said.

CHAPTER THIRTEEN

Robert swam to the ladder and climbed up halfway, allowing the water to drain from his clothes. "How'd you find me?"

"Ms. Lavinia told me your plan," Glenn said. "Did you get the key?"

"Not yet."

"Did you look in the study?"

Robert dragged himself out of the pool and collapsed onto the deck. "I tried," he said, "but first I was captured by a giant blob of green jelly. Then I was tied to a chair and a bug monster puked on my ankles. And then I had to run away from Miss Mandis, because apparently she's a bug monster, too."

"Oh," Glenn said. "Why didn't you ask me for help?"

"Because you told me to leave you alone," Robert reminded him. "Because, for the past two days, you've been acting like a real jerk."

Glenn muttered something that sounded like an apology.

"Why didn't you tell me your mother was home?"

"It's only temporary."

"What's that mean?"

"She does this every year. She comes home, she brings me new clothes, she and my dad are happy, everything's perfect. But it never lasts. You'll see. In a few days, they'll start fighting again and then she'll be back in Arizona. I guarantee it."

"What about the baby?"

"She'll go back with my mom. She's my little sister and I barely know her."

"You should've just told me," Robert said.

"I figured I would ignore you until she and my sister went away. And then you'd never know they'd been here."

Glenn was staring down at the swimming pool, and Robert realized his friend was ashamed. All this time, he was acting weird because he was ashamed.

"So you're *not* a zombie?"

"What?"

"That wasp sting? The boil on the back of your neck? It wasn't controlling your brain or anything?"

"No," Glenn said, laughing. He pulled back his collar so Robert could see the welt. It had shrunk to the size of a mosquito bite; in another day or so, it would be completely gone. "It's just my stupid messed-up family, that's all."

Robert crossed his arms over his chest. He was still soaking wet and starting to shiver. Fortunately, he had a change of clothes in the locker room.

"Well, at least your mom's trying," he pointed out. "She comes back every year. I've never even met my dad."

Glenn looked up. It was the first time Robert had ever mentioned his father. "Where does your dad live?"

"We have no idea. I don't know anything about him. He took off before I was born. But don't tell anybody, all right?"

Robert hadn't shared this information with many people, but he felt his best friend deserved to know. Glenn wasn't the only person ashamed of his stupid, messed-up family.

"At least your mom's cool," Glenn said.

"She's been asking about you. She wants to know when you're coming back to dinner."

"Next week at the latest. I guarantee it."

The fourth-period bell rang and Robert jumped up. He still needed to dry off and change before heading to language arts class. "I better go. Mr. Loomis is going to bust me for being late."

Glenn followed him to the boys' locker room. "Hold up," he called. "I still haven't told you my good news."

"There's good news?"

"Yeah. While you were running around Tillinghast Mansion, I found a way into the basement." He clapped his best friend on the shoulder. "Soon as school's over, we're getting your rats back."

CHAPTER FOURTEEN

Robert was ten minutes late to language arts, and his classmates laughed when he arrived dressed in his gym clothes: sweatpants, a T-shirt, and a nylon windbreaker.

Mr. Loomis was standing at the chalkboard, preparing to announce the latest reading assignment. Instead of yelling at Robert, he seemed concerned. "Is everything all right? Why is your hair wet?"

Robert just apologized for being late and hurried to his seat.

Mr. Loomis was Robert's favorite teacher at Lovecraft Middle School, even though he had a reputation for being a bit of a goofball. He wore pastel-colored sweater vests every day of the week, and he was always raving about great books and the joys of reading.

"We're starting a new novel today and it's one of my favorites," he explained. "It's about a group of British schoolchildren stranded on a tropical island. Every page is packed with action and adventure." He began distributing paperback copies to students in the front row. "It's my tremendous pleasure to introduce *Lord of the Flies*!"

The door to the classroom opened and Howard Mergler entered on his forearm crutches, slowly click-clacking across the room. "Sorry I'm late," he said. "I had a little trouble coming up the stairs."

"No need to apologize, Howard," Mr. Loomis replied. "In fact, I think this school owes you a debt of gratitude. I haven't seen a single insect all day!" He started clapping, and this time all the students joined in without being prompted. Everyone was glad to have the bugs out of the school.

"There's no need to thank me," Howard said. "As your student council president, I'm always happy to serve you." He was addressing the class but looking straight at Robert. "All the insects have been destroyed, so we can stop worrying about them and focus on our schoolwork. That's the most important thing, right, Mr. Loomis?"

Their teacher seemed genuinely touched by the speech. "Absolutely correct," he said. "Let's all get back to learning."

Mr. Loomis resumed his lesson, distributing copies of *Lord of the Flies* and describing the novel's major themes. Robert found it hard to concentrate on the discussion. He kept staring at the clock, watching the minutes tick by. Three-fifteen couldn't come fast enough. He couldn't wait to hear Glenn's plan for rescuing Pip and Squeak.

From out of nowhere, a small square of folded loose-leaf paper flicked onto his desk.

Someone had passed him a note.

He glanced around the classroom, hoping to identify the person who sent it. All the students were facing forward, their eyes on Mr. Loomis and the chalkboard. All except Howard Mergler, who had a sinister grin on his face.

Robert waited until the teacher turned his back, then carefully unwrapped the note. A black powder spilled onto his desk. It looked like a teaspoon's worth of ground pepper. Robert turned the paper over, but both sides were blank. If someone was trying to send him a message, he certainly didn't understand it.

Again he looked around the classroom. Howard's smile was wider than ever. Mr. Loomis was still describing the major themes of *Lord of the Flies*, and kids were writing the ideas in their notebooks. No one seemed to notice the pepper grains scattered across Robert's desk.

And then, to his astonishment, one of the grains jumped two feet in the air. It landed in the hair of Eileen Moore, the girl sitting in front of him. Another speck leapt even higher, soaring across the classroom. Robert studied the little mound of pepper more carefully and realized it was a swarm of fleas. One by one, the insects were vaulting off his desk in all directions, landing on the hair and collars and clothes of his class-mates. The fleas were so tiny that no one even noticed. Within seconds, the entire swarm had scattered.

"Robert Arthur!" Mr. Loomis shouted, pointing to the sheet of loose-leaf paper. "Please tell me you're not passing notes. Is that something you'd like to share with the entire class?"

Robert shook his head. *I just did*, he thought.

CHAPTER FIFTEEN

Three-fifteen finally came, and Robert ran to meet Glenn in the school auditorium. The space was as grand and majestic as any Broadway theater, with a curtained stage and enough seating for an audience of seven hundred. In the center of the ceiling was a large dome, currently under reconstruction. A few weeks earlier, its glass had been shattered after Robert unwittingly summoned a giant harpy during a student council debate.

Glenn was waiting in the front row.

"Why are we meeting here?" Robert asked. "This is nowhere near the basement."

"Let me explain," Glenn said. "I've been thinking

about the ventilation ducts. Basically, they carry heat from the basement and deliver it all over the school. But some rooms need more heat than others, right?"

"I guess," Robert said.

"A tiny room like the nurse's office needs a tiny amount of heat, so it has a tiny vent. But a bigger classroom needs a bigger vent. And a giant auditorium needs a giant vent . . . one that's big enough for a person to climb through."

Glenn stepped aside, revealing a large slatted vent at the base of the stage. He had already removed the screws so Robert could peer inside. Behind the vent was a cramped metal tunnel, eighteen inches high and stretching into the darkness.

"You're a genius," Robert said, grinning. "Do you think this goes all the way to the basement?"

"There's only one way to find out," Glenn said. "Are you coming with me?"

"Absolutely not!" a distant voice exclaimed.

Ms. Lavinia had entered the auditorium through the backstage entrance, and now she was crossing the stage. Her shrill voice echoed throughout the theater. Karina Ortiz trailed a few steps behind, carrying her skateboard.

"Why not?" Glenn asked.

"It's far too dangerous," Ms. Lavinia insisted. "We've already lost the rats. If anything happens to you—"

"Nothing's going to happen," Glenn said.

"You have no idea, Mr. Torkells." The librarian only used their last names when she was extremely upset. "We are talking about thousands of insects. Dozens of different species. What if they joined forces and attacked you simultaneously?"

Glenn reached into his coat pocket for his secret weapon: a large aerosol spray can of Dead Bug. "'One blast kills virtually anything,'" he said, reading aloud from the label. "'Ants, bees, flies, wasps . . .'"

"And people!" Ms. Lavinia exclaimed, snatching the can from his hands. "Are you crazy? If you spray this garbage inside the ducts, you'll poison yourself and the entire school. Absolutely not."

Karina remained silent. Robert hadn't seen her since two nights earlier, when he lost his temper and called her a ghost. She wouldn't even look at him.

"Karina?" he asked. "Can I talk to you about something?"

She shrugged. "Go ahead. Talk."

"In private," Robert said.

Grudgingly, she followed him to the back of the auditorium. Ms. Lavinia didn't even notice—she was still lecturing Glenn on the stupidity of spraying bug poison into the school ventilation system.

"I'm sorry I called you a ghost," Robert said. "I know you don't like that word. And I didn't mean to hurt your feelings. It was right after Pip and Squeak disappeared, and I was scared."

"I know," Karina said. "I was scared, too."

"The first couple times I met you, I didn't even realize you were . . . not living. Do you remember?"

"I remember."

"I never thought of you that way. I still don't. When we're hanging out and stuff, I think of you as a regular, ordinary girl."

"Ordinary?"

"Totally ordinary," he insisted. "If we were strangers? And I saw you standing in a crowd of other kids? I wouldn't even notice you."

"That's very sweet," Karina said, shaking her head. "That's probably the nicest thing you've ever said to me."

"So you're not mad anymore?"

"I was never mad. I'm just frustrated, that's all. I'm tired of being trapped in this place."

"We have fun hanging out, don't we?" Robert asked.

"Yeah, but in a few years, you'll be in high school. You'll have a driver's license. And I'll still be stuck here and I'll still be thirteen. Will you like hanging out with me then?"

"Of course I will."

"I don't think so."

"Look, I'll probably be a ghost myself," Robert assured her. "If Tillinghast gets his way, Glenn and I will be dead before I leave this place. And then the three of us can hang out all the time."

Karina scowled. "That's not even funny," she said, and all of a sudden she seemed angry again. "You don't *ever* want to be stuck here. You'd hate it, and I'd spend the rest of eternity blaming myself."

With that, she abruptly returned to the front of the auditorium, where Glenn and Ms. Lavinia were still arguing.

"I'm going with the boys," Karina announced. "They need my help."

Ms. Lavinia frowned. "Now *you* think this is a good idea?"

"We owe it to Pip and Squeak. We sent them into the vents and told them everything would be fine. They trusted us."

"The basement will be full of insects," Robert reminded her. "You hate insects."

"I only hate spiders," Karina reminded him. "Technically, they're not insects. They're arachnids."

"Same difference." Back when they first met, Robert, Glenn, and Karina shared a close call with a giant spider and thousands of spiderlings in Tillinghast Mansion. But whatever was waiting in the school basement was likely to be much, much worse.

"The bugs can't touch me, and I can't touch them," Karina said. "As long as I remember that, I'll be fine. I want to do this." She turned to Ms. Lavinia. "Please let us do this."

Against her better judgment, Ms. Lavinia stepped away from the vent. "Keep your voices down," she warned. "Any sounds you make will echo through the school."

Glenn crawled into the duct first, followed by Robert and then Karina. Once they were all inside, Ms. Lavinia replaced the vent cover and screwed it in place. "Be careful," she said.

Right from the beginning, moving through the duct was much harder than any of them had imagined. It wasn't big enough for Robert to crawl on all fours. He had to creep forward in tiny increments, pushing off with his sneakers and "walking" with his elbows. It was hard work; he was using muscles he didn't normally use, muscles he wasn't even aware he had. After ten minutes, he was exhausted.

"You guys need to be more quiet," Karina said. "You're making a racket."

"I can't help it," Glenn told her.

"Are we almost there?" Robert asked.

Glenn laughed. "Look behind you."

There was barely enough room for Robert to turn his head and shoulders. Karina was directly behind him, and just beyond her was the vent cover. Robert was still close enough to see Ms. Lavinia watching them through the slats.

They had barely traveled twenty feet.

CHAPTER SIXTEEN

So they crawled.

And crawled and crawled, and then crawled some more.

This is how it feels to be a bug, Robert thought. A person could walk the entire length of Lovecraft Middle School in about five minutes. But here in the ducts, down on his belly, advancing just two inches at a time, that same journey was going to take all afternoon.

Even worse, the ducts were stifling hot. Robert felt as if he was in an oven and soon wished he had removed his jacket. Sweat dripped down his forehead and stung his eyes. The only relief came when they passed beneath one of the large circular fans, spaced every twenty feet or so. A warm breeze was better than no breeze at all.

Sometimes, the duct would fork, and the three of them would stop to discuss the best way forward. Sometimes they passed vents offering views into classrooms and offices; they learned that this particular duct brought heat to Principal Slater's office, the cafeteria, and a space that appeared to be the faculty lounge. Occasionally, they would hear or see a teacher working late, and Glenn would give the signal to freeze. Then they would all lie silent and wait until the teacher moved on.

After more than an hour of crawling, the duct finally widened into a sort of hub. Five other ducts extended from there, like spokes on a wheel. Robert, Glenn, and Karina had just enough room to sit up and face one another.

"Which way?" Robert asked.

Not one of them had any idea.

"We must be getting close," Karina said.

Glenn aimed his flashlight into the different passages.

Each one looked identical. Robert felt as if he was in one of those cornfield mazes where every path looked exactly the same; there was no way for him to orient himself. At this rate, they would be trapped behind the walls all night.

"This one," Karina pointed.

To Robert and Glenn, it seemed like she had chosen at random.

"How do you know?" Robert asked.

"Take a whiff," Karina said.

Robert placed his head in the duct, inhaled deeply, and immediately wished he hadn't. It smelled like the back of a garbage truck.

"Oh, man, that reeks!" Glenn exclaimed.

"It must be the food supply," Karina said. "All those bugs have to be eating something."

"And if we find the food supply, I bet we find Pip and Squeak," Robert said. "Let's go."

Glenn pulled the front of his shirt up and over his nose and then led the way into the passage. Until this point, the crawling had been merely uncomfortable.

Now, with the stink of rotten garbage, it became un-bearable—and the more they crawled, the worse the odor grew.

Yet they were definitely on the right track. After another few minutes in the cramped passage, Glenn announced that they had company. Sure enough, Robert felt a housefly land on his arm. Then another and another. Here and there on the sides of the vent were tiny white blobs, what appeared to be larvae.

"Every time I think this can't get more disgusting," Karina said, "the school finds new ways to surprise me."

"They can't touch you, and you can't touch them," Robert reminded her.

"But they're all touching me," Glenn chimed in.

Five o'clock came and went, and still they were only creeping along. A swarm of black flies had set-tled on Robert's head, shoulders, and back. He'd stopped shaking them off—there were too many and they were relentless. He realized he wasn't going to be home in time for dinner, that his mother would be wor-ried sick, but what could he do? He was beginning to think they would be trapped inside the stifling vents forever.

"Uh-oh," Glenn said.

"Uh-oh what?" Robert asked apprehensively.

They had reached a three-foot gap. It looked remarkably similar to the chasm that had swallowed Pip and Squeak, and Robert realized he was facing their same predicament. The passage continued on the other side of the gap, but there was no way they could make it across. They couldn't leap very far while crawling on their hands and knees.

Glenn pointed his flashlight into the chasm, and all three looked down. The airshaft dropped more than twenty feet into darkness.

"The basement's down there," Karina said. "It has to be."

"Anybody bring a rope?" Glenn asked.

"I wish," Robert said.

They had only three options, and none of them were good: Leaping across the chasm to other side was impossible. Backtracking through the vents to the auditorium would take hours. And dropping into a bottomless pit was the worst choice of all. It meant falling to an all-but-certain death.

"We're stuck," Robert said.

"You're forgetting about me," Karina said. "I can go check it out. If it's safe when I get to the bottom, I'll call up and let you know."

"And if it's not?" Robert asked.

"What's the worst that could happen?"

On a purely logical level, Robert knew Karina was right—it's not like she could die twice. But all the same, the idea of her jumping into a bottomless pit made him nervous. Anything could be waiting down there. There was no telling what Howard and Tillinghast had planned for the basement.

"I'll be fine," Karina assured him. "Make some room."

She squeezed past the two boys, crawling up to the precipice and diving over the edge headfirst. Her figure vanished into the darkness without a sound. As the moments slowly passed, Robert started to worry that they'd made a terrible miscalculation. Maybe Karina *could* die twice. Or maybe, in the basement of Lovecraft Middle School, lurked a fate even worse than death—

Then her voice rose out of the darkness:

"All right."

Glenn insisted on a little more information. He leaned over the edge and shouted into the void. "What do you mean, 'all right'? What's down there?"

"You can jump." Karina's voice was tinny and soft; it sounded like it was a million miles away. "You won't get hurt."

"Why not? What's down there?"

"Um . . . you'll see. Just keep your mouths closed."

Glenn and Robert exchanged nervous glances: *Keep your mouths closed?*

"I'll go first," Robert volunteered.

He swung his legs over the edge of the chasm and dropped feetfirst. The fall lasted only a few seconds, but time seemed to pass in slow motion. The aluminum panels of the duct blurred past. Flies pinged off his face and hands, as if he were flying through a dense swarm. As he reached the bottom the airshaft grew brighter and brighter, and then he was sailing out of the vent, dropping from the ceiling into a large subterranean room. And the whole time Robert was afraid to look down. He feared that—despite Karina's promises—he would see a solid concrete floor rushing up to meet him.

Instead, he landed on a cloud.

Or at least that's what it felt like—this soft, spongy surface that absorbed the impact of his fall. Robert sat up and looked around. He was in the basement mechanical room—and he was up to his waist in a Dumpster full of wet rice.

"Get out!" Karina yelled. She was standing on the side of the garbage bin, gesturing for Robert to move as quickly as possible, but he didn't understand the urgency.

"I'm fine," he said. "That didn't even hurt."

"Keep your mouth shut," she said. "Just get out!"

"What's the big deal? It's only garbage."

And the garbage wasn't even particularly disgust-ing. Here and there were moldy peaches, apple cores, and other rotting fruits, but most of the bin was filled with white rice.

Many thousands of grains of squirming white rice.

Robert's eyes narrowed.

Maggots.

CHAPTER
SEVENTEEN

Robert leapt out of the garbage, shrieking and shouting and swatting the larvae from his clothes, neck, and hair. They were everywhere—inside his sneakers, behind his ears, under his collar. They clung to his skin like tiny leeches.

"I'm sorry," Karina told him. "I figured it was better if you didn't know."

Glenn dropped into the garbage a moment later—and unfortunately he ignored Karina's warning to keep his mouth closed. Worse, he screamed "Yahoooo!" all the way down and ended up swallowing some larvae. He spent the next few minutes spitting on the basement floor, trying to rid his mouth of their awful bitter taste. "This is the most disgusting thing that's ever happened to us," he said, groaning.

"Stick around," Robert told him. "We're not finished yet."

"Look on the bright side," Karina said. "At least we're out of the ducts."

They looked around. The mechanical room was a labyrinth of giant steel pipelines, plastic tubes, and metal ducts that appeared to deliver heat, cold air, and water all throughout the building. The room was alive with the buzzing of boilers, handlers, pumps, and generators.

"So, this is it?" Glenn asked. "This is the giant underground burrow?"

"It's too bright," Karina said.

"What do you mean?"

"Have you ever walked into the woods and flipped over a rock? You know all the weird slithery bugs that cling to the bottom? The bugs that like cool, dark places? That's the kind of space we're looking for. They're going to be hiding."

"Howard said the entrance was well-concealed," Robert remembered. "He said not even the janitors would be able to find it."

They spread out across the mechanical room, checking every corner. Robert crawled under boilers; Glenn squeezed behind air compressors; Karina searched in supply closets. Everything was neat and clean and orderly. Apart from the swarms of flies, there were no signs of anything amiss.

At the far end of the basement was a window overlooking a much smaller adjacent room; a sign on the door read POOL UTILITY. Robert glanced through the window but saw nothing unusual, only several fifty-five-gallon barrels of liquid chlorine, stockpiled in the corner. He was turning away when he stepped on something small and brittle.

He leapt back, thinking he had crushed some kind of hard-shelled beetle. But no—it was the frayed end of a yellow USB cable.

"That's the wire!" Karina exclaimed. "Remember the cameras Pip and Squeak were wearing?"

Robert lifted the cable. Karina was right—it was the same yellow wire that Ms. Lavinia had affixed to the camera helmet, the same yellow wire that had disappeared through the ventilation ducts. "It was a hundred feet long," Robert said. "If Pip and Squeak are still attached to the other end, they must be close."

All three followed the cable out of the mechanical room and into the pool utility room, where it disappeared among the jumble of barrels. It took ten minutes of shoving and grunting before the boys moved the containers aside and discovered a small hole in the wall. It wasn't like the ventilation duct; this opening definitely wasn't man-made. It looked like it had been gnawed on by a variety of creatures, and the yellow wire disappeared through its center.

Glenn aimed his flashlight inside. The passage descended into the earth, as if it had been dug by a mole or a groundhog. "*Another* tunnel?"

"This is more like it," Karina said. "This is where we'll find some bugs."

Robert knew she was right. "Howard said the

burrow was underneath the soccer field. We have to crawl out of the school to get there."

He wriggled into the opening headfirst. On a class trip back in third grade, Robert had toured an underground cavern; he found the insect burrow had the same cool temperature, the same dank smell, the same overwhelming sense of blackness. The passage was hollowed out of dirt and clay, and roots and stones jutted in from the sides.

"Come on," he called back. "We're getting close."

The tunnel began as a tight squeeze but quickly expanded to a height that allowed them to stand. Glenn's flashlight did little to illuminate the darkness, but they saw a faint orange glow in the distance.

"How much farther?" Karina asked.

Robert was coiling the wire around his wrist, and he estimated he had collected most of it. "Maybe another thirty feet," he said. "We're almost there."

The ground sloped upward, and they arrived in a large circular chamber. The walls were ringed with torches providing heat so the insects could thrive.

And they certainly were thriving. Termites and butterflies coated the ceiling. Grasshoppers and millipedes clung to the walls. The floor was teeming with bugs upon bugs—locusts on top of caterpillars on top of katydids. Robert avoided looking down and ignored the disgusting crunch of his footsteps.

As he pulled the last few inches of wire through his hands, he found it stretching up to the ceiling—to a silky white cocoon tethered to the earthen wall.

Karina gasped. "Oh, no."

Robert knew what she was thinking. Some spiders cocooned their prey before eating them. It was a way of storing their meals for a later time—the spider equivalent of stashing leftovers in the fridge. Robert yanked on the wire, hoping to pull down the entire cocoon.

Instead, the opposite end of the wire simply popped out. Attached were the helmets and leather glove that Ms. Lavinia had stitched together in the library. The materials looked corroded, as if they had been partially digested.

"That doesn't mean anything," Glenn insisted. "We need to get them down. There's a chance they're still OK."

Inside the burrow was one of the fifty-five-gallon drums, lying on its side. It was full of crickets and moths and other bugs that liked to nest in dark, shadowy places. Glenn rolled it across the floor, slapping away the insects that scrambled across its surface. He stopped underneath the cocoon, then flipped the drum upright and hammered the lid on top. "This ought to hold me, don't you think?"

"I'll do it," Robert said.

"I'm taller," Glenn reminded him. "It'll be easier for me to reach them."

"But they're my pets. I got them into this mess."

"At least let me give you a boost." Glenn knelt down and formed his hands into a step. "Come on."

Robert climbed up to the top of the barrel. It wobbled from side to side on the uneven dirt floor, and he paused to steady his balance. He still wasn't tall enough to reach the cocoon, but if he used the handle of the flashlight, he could manage to tap it.

"Guys?" he whispered. "Can you hear me?"

No answer.

He tapped it again, harder this time.

The cocoon broke away from the wall and fell to the ground.

It was perfectly still.

"Oh, Robert," Karina said. "I am so sorry."

CHAPTER
EIGHTEEN

Robert couldn't believe it. All this time, while he was crawling through the vents and slapping bugs off his face and plucking maggots out of his earlobes, all this time he was convinced that Pip and Squeak were fine. He had believed he only needed to find them. He never considered they would be . . .

It was unthinkable.

The cocoon was light and extremely brittle, and it reminded Robert of the papier-mâché projects he'd made in art class. He gave it a little rattle, hoping to feel something stirring inside. But the cocoon was lifeless.

"Well, I'm not leaving them here," he said. "I won't

let them be lunch for a bunch of stupid bugs. I'll take them home and bury them."

"That's a good idea," Karina said. She was already blinking back tears. "You can bury them under your bedroom window. They were always happiest in your house."

As they turned to leave, they heard voices coming from the entrance of the burrow.

"Oh, this is wonderful, wonderful!"

"Yes, Master is very pleased with me."

Robert grabbed the cocoon and ducked behind the barrel. "Over here," he called, and Glenn and Karina squeezed in beside him. The drum wasn't big enough to conceal all three of them, but the shadows at the edge of the dark underground space helped to hide them.

Howard Mergler and Miss Mandis entered the burrow, carrying trash bags full of moldy peaches and rotten banana peels. Together, they flung the fruit across the room.

"Come and eat, my brothers and sisters!" Howard

exclaimed. "Your master commands you!"

"Eat, grow, and multiply!" Miss Mandis cried. "Your bodies must be strong for the Great War!"

As Robert crouched behind the barrel, he became acutely aware of the beetles and cockroaches walking over his sneakers, of the crickets and termites and stinkbugs clinging to the walls. The insects were clicking their jaws and beating their wings, trying to draw attention to the intruders, but Howard and Miss Mandis were too caught up in their crazy pep rally to notice.

"For centuries, the humans have trampled us! Squashed us! Swatted us! Poisoned us!" Howard exclaimed. "But this spring, with Master's help, you will have your revenge!"

Robert felt the pitter-patter of tiny feet creeping up his back, over his neck, and into his hair. It was either a lot of little bugs or one giant bug with a lot of little legs. He couldn't decide which was worse.

"Don't move," Glenn whispered.

Robert glanced over. A greasy brown cockroach

crawled over Glenn's ear, walked across his cheek, and tickled his nose with its antennae. Moths were fluttering around Karina's forehead, trying but failing to nest in her hair. The bugs were intent on scaring the friends out of the shadows, but they refused to budge.

"When the snow thaws, we will no longer live in the cracks and crevasses of society!" Miss Mandis cried. "We will no longer hide beneath rocks!"

Robert felt a red-hot pinprick on the back of his neck—and then another and another. It felt like staples were being fired into his skin. Something was biting him. A tingling sensation began coursing through his bloodstream. The bugs were also biting Glenn, and probably trying to bite Karina, too, but none of them flinched. They knew they only needed to endure a few more minutes of pain. Howard and Miss Mandis had emptied their feedbag and were now dumping the last few scraps on the ground.

"Be strong, my brothers and sisters!" Howard cried.

"We will return in the morning with more nourishment!" Miss Mandis promised. "Farewell!"

They were turning to leave when all the shadows surrounding Robert vanished. Suddenly the walls were illuminated by a ghastly green light. He looked up and saw dozens of fireflies hovering above his head. Their glowing tails formed a signal that couldn't be ignored.

Robert and his friends stood up, realizing there was no point in hiding anymore.

"Intruders!" Miss Mandis shrieked.

"You shouldn't be down here," Howard said. "This entire basement is off-limits to students."

"It's too late," Robert said. "We already know your plan. We know all about the army you're building."

"Yeah," Glenn said, "and we're going to tell everyone. They'll bring in real exterminators with real poison. They'll fumigate the whole place."

Howard's shirt split along its seams as two long wings burst from his back and rose above his shoulders. "You're not telling anyone," he said. "You're going straight to Tillinghast Mansion, and you'll surrender your vessels once and for all!"

Spiky bristles sprouted from his face, and huge

compound eyes erupted from the sides of his head. It looked like a metamorphosis, but really he was just shedding his human skin and revealing his true arthropod form. A second pair of segmented limbs unfurled from his torso, and his hideous vertical mandibles clacked with laughter.

Karina turned to Robert. "Remember when I said I only hated spiders? And other bugs didn't bother me very much?"

"Yeah?"

"I was wrong about that."

The burrow had just one exit, and the shaggai was blocking it. He waved his four upper limbs menacingly, daring Robert and his friends to get past him.

"Sit down, children," Miss Mandis told them, "and we'll promise not to hurt you too much."

Robert thought back to earlier in the day, when he had struggled with Miss Mandis outside Tillinghast Mansion. He remembered that she wasn't strong enough to keep him from leaping into the pond.

And then he remembered what Miss Lynch had

taught the class during homeroom: *the average adult housefly weighs remarkably little . . . less than a cotton ball.*

He had nothing to lose. He gripped the cocoon tightly and charged toward the shaggai with his head down, slamming his shoulder into its thorax. To his astonishment, it was like tackling a department store mannequin. The arthropod fell to the ground, all six limbs flailing wildly, and Robert kept running.

His friends followed behind him.

"Dude, that was awesome!" Glenn said. "How'd you know that would work?"

"I pay attention in class," Robert said. "You should try it sometime."

Miss Mandis wasn't even trying to stop them. She just kept chanting *"S'von delagos! S'von delagos!"* over and over. It sounded like a cry for help.

"What's she saying?" Glenn asked.

"I don't know," Karina said.

"Why isn't she following us?"

"Just keep moving."

They scrambled through the tunnel and emerged in the pool utility room, crawling past the storage drums. All they needed to do was open the door to the mechanical room and head upstairs to the school . . .

But the door was blocked by a huge cloud of wasps—hundreds of them, with long wings and spiked purple abdomens, all buzzing loudly.

"Uh-oh," Glenn said.

Now Robert understood why Miss Mandis hadn't bothered following them. They were already trapped. One sting from a wasp had been bad enough. Dozens of stings would be fatal.

"What do we do?" Karina asked.

"I don't know," Robert said.

He tucked the cocoon under his shirt to keep it safe. Then he took off his windbreaker and waved it like a cape, snapping it at the wasps, keeping them back. He knew it was a desperate move; no windbreaker in the world would be big enough to stop them. He needed a better weapon, something that could take down all of them at once. He needed—

"Water!" Karina shouted.

She pointed to the pool filtration system in the corner of the room; in its center was a large wheel valve used to divert water away from the filter.

"Open it!" Karina explained. "You can spray them!"

Robert grabbed the wheel, but it didn't budge. He wasn't strong enough. A wasp buzzed toward his head, and he ducked away from the attack just in time.

Glenn hurried over, and both of them tried together. The wheel turned a few inches, enough to unleash a torrent of chlorinated water. Within seconds, hundreds of gallons blasted across the room. The wasps flew in all directions, trying to avoid the spray, but it was too big and too fast. Their wings, soaked and heavy, soon grounded the entire swarm.

"All right, that's enough!" Karina shouted. "Turn it off!"

Robert and Glenn tried to spin the wheel in the opposite direction, but their fingers slipped along its surface; their hands were too wet to grip the slick metal.

Somewhere above them, a siren was blaring—the drain had triggered some kind of alarm.

"We need to go!" Glenn shouted.

"We can't leave the water running," Karina said. "It'll drain the whole swimming pool. You'll flood the entire basement!"

That gave Robert an idea. "We won't flood the basement," he said. "We'll flood the burrow!"

There was a large round grate in the middle of the floor, meant to drain the water in precisely this kind of emergency. Robert took his windbreaker and placed it over the drain, immediately clogging it. The water, already ankle deep, began rising even faster.

"Hurry!" Robert shouted to Glenn. "Get the door!"

The door to the mechanical room swung inward, and too much standing water would make it impossible to open. Glenn struggled to pull it against the rising tide. Karina and Robert squeezed through, then Glenn followed, and the door slammed shut.

Safe and dry on the other side, they watched through the window as water filled the pool utility room. Within a minute, it was waist high and rushing into the burrow. The insects inside were trapped—as were Howard and Miss Mandis. The entire underground cavern was about to become an underwater grave.

The siren continued to blare, loud and shrill.

"We should go," Karina said. "The police will be coming."

All three ran up the stairs to the first floor. Luckily, the door to the mechanical room was locked only from the inside, and they had no trouble opening it. Together they ran down the central corridor toward the school's main entrance—but as they approached, they realized it was too late. Police cars and a fire truck were already waiting in front of the building, and Principal Slater was unlocking the doors.

They turned and ran in the opposite direction.

"Who's there?" Principal Slater called. "Stop right this instant!"

Robert heard boots hitting the ground, running behind them. He and Glenn and Karina were quickly approaching the end of the hallway, which forked in two directions.

"We need to split up," Karina said. "You and Glenn go through the gym. I'll lead them the other way."

"What if they catch you?"

She grinned. "No one's going to catch me. I'm a ghost, remember?" Robert was surprised to hear the word come out of Karina's mouth, but she no longer seemed ashamed of it. She seemed to finally understand that it made no difference to Robert either way. "Now go on, hurry!"

Glenn didn't need to be told twice. He was already racing through the gym. Robert ran after him while Karina lingered in the hallway, ready to lure the grown-ups in the opposite direction. "Thanks," he called.

"Don't thank me," she called back. "Just run!"

CHAPTER

NINETEEN

The boys raced through the locker room and sprinted outside onto the athletic fields. The stadium lights were off, and the grounds of the school were completely dark.

Glenn pointed to the far end of the soccer field, which was bordered by a thick tangle of woods. "We'll cut through there," he said. "If anyone follows us, we'll lose them in the trees."

But Robert realized something was wrong. The grass on the field was wet and muddy, even though it hadn't rained in nearly a week. He felt like he was running across soft, spongy marshmallow; in some places, his sneakers sank six inches into the ground.

"What's going on?" Glenn asked.

"I don't know—"

Suddenly the field ruptured and Robert sank to his waist in dirty water. He held tight to the cocoon and gripped the sides of the earth with his free hand, trying to hoist himself out even as the muddy ground collapsed around him.

At first he thought it was an earthquake. The soccer field appeared to be cratering. Water was gurgling up out of the ground. Then Robert smelled chlorine and immediately realized what was happening.

The burrow was bursting.

The soccer field was just a thin skin across its surface, and now it was sinking into a giant underground lake. The water churned like an ocean at high tide; dead or drowning bugs were floating everywhere, thousands of them, flies and beetles, spiders and centipedes. Robert would have to swim to survive; he had to let go of the cocoon. The silk strands were melting, dissolving like cotton candy, revealing the mummified corpses of his pets. He looked down at Pip and Squeak for a final farewell.

"I'm sorry, guys," he said. "This was all my fault."

Squeak seemed to twitch his whiskers, and Robert thought it was just his imagination. But then Pip opened his eyes halfway and shook his head. *It's not your fault*, the rat seemed to be saying.

"Wait, you heard that?" he asked.

This time, Pip nodded. Squeak opened his eyes, and the rats managed to wag their tail. Robert quickly checked their body for cuts or bites. Their fur was matted with gunk, but it seemed the helmets and homemade glove-coat had protected them from any serious injuries. The water was still raging all around them, and Robert was struggling to stay afloat. He placed the rats on his shoulder, explaining to them, "I need you to hang on while I swim. Can you do that?"

He felt a familiar tug on his shoulder as the rats dug in with their claws.

"Look out!" Glenn shouted.

A fifty-five-gallon barrel erupted from the churning sea, casting giant waves that nearly struck Robert in the face. He kicked his legs, treading water, doing his best to keep Pip and Squeak above the surface.

With an ear-splitting screech, Miss Mandis rose out of the lake, clawing at her skin and shedding her human disguise. Her true face was green, triangular, and studded with large compound eyes. Her angular limbs ended in bladed tips that made swimming impossible; she scrambled to pull herself onto the top of the barrel, which was floating like a life raft.

She saw Robert and shrieked. "You've ruined everything! Our entire army, destroyed!"

Robert realized she was unable to swim after him—that she was unable to swim at all. He paddled away from her as Pip and Squeak clung to his shoulder. *Just hang on a little longer*, he promised them. *I'm going to get you out of here.*

A moment later, the shaggai broke through the water's surface. His spindly limbs and heavy wings made him equally ill-suited for swimming. He reached toward Miss Mandis's barrel, and she slashed at him with her bladed limbs.

"Stay back!" she warned. "You're too heavy!"

"I'm sinking!"

"Find your own barrel!"

But there were no other barrels, at least none that Robert could see. He knew that only the empty barrel had risen to the surface because it was buoyant enough to float.

"Move over!" the shaggai growled.

"Let go!" Miss Mandis shrieked, flicking her forelimb at his head. "You'll sink us both!"

The shaggai ignored her threats. He reached for the top of the drum, trying to pull himself up as Miss Mandis chopped at his thorax. He bellowed in pain, sliding off but clinging to the lid to stay afloat.

"Not the lid!" Miss Mandis cried.

But it was too late. The shaggai's grip was strong. The lid popped off and water rushed to fill the void. Miss Mandis shrieked as her life raft capsized.

"No!" she shouted. "Nooooo!"

The two creatures clung to each other, as if together they might keep themselves from sinking, but it

was no use. A wave swept over their heads, and they disappeared beneath the churning waters.

Glenn swam over to help Robert. "Are you OK?"

"I think so."

"Come on. Let's get out of here."

The boys reached the far end of the field, dragged themselves up on the muddy shore, and then turned to study the wreckage. The water had finally stopped churning and settled to a state of calm. The new lake was enormous, spanning the entire soccer field. Thousands of bloated bugs bobbed on its surface.

Beyond the lake, police officers and firefighters were emerging from the school, pointing their flashlights at the strange body of water that had mysteriously appeared behind Lovecraft Middle School. The boys ducked behind the trees and escaped into the woods. Robert lifted Pip and Squeak off his shoulder and carried them in the safety of his arms.

Glenn studied the rats in disbelief.

"They're alive," he said.

"I knew you would be," Robert whispered to his

pets. "This whole time, I always knew you would be."
He scratched the backs of their necks, assuring them
that everything was going to be all right, and both of
his rats quietly chattered their teeth.

CHAPTER
TWENTY

In the end, everything was blamed on the janitors.

If they had been doing their jobs, people said, the insect population never would have exploded. The pool drain never would have malfunctioned. The soccer field never would have collapsed into a giant underground lake.

And, most important, Howard Mergler and Miss Mandis never would have died.

It was widely believed that the student council president and school nurse had somehow drowned in the flood, though their bodies had yet to be recovered. Professional scuba divers made several trips to the bottom of the lake, searching for human remains, to no avail. All they could find were thousands of dead insects and bug parts. In her official statement to the media, Principal Slater admitted, "We may never know the truth of what happened here."

In the days to come, life at Lovecraft Middle School gradually returned to normal. There were no more flies in the hallway; there were no more pill bugs in the cafeteria food. The winter weather made it impossible for any insects to survive for very long. Already the new lake on the soccer field was freezing over, and students were asking if it could be used for skating and ice hockey. Best of all, everyone's hair was growing back—the Lovecraft lice epidemic had finally come to an end.

On Friday night, one week after all the craziness ended, Robert sat down with his mother for dinner. They were having chicken tacos, Robert's favorite.

"So," Mrs. Arthur asked, "how's seventh grade treating you?"

He smiled. "Fantastic."

"Really? What happened today?"

"Absolutely nothing," Robert said. "I just went to class, listened to my teachers, and learned stuff."

Mrs. Arthur was surprised. "That sounds like a normal, regular day."

"Exactly," he said. "It was terrific."

When his mother wasn't looking, Robert broke a taco shell in his lap and pushed the pieces inside his pockets. Pip and Squeak loved taco shells. The rats had spent the past few days upstairs in his bedroom, snoozing in the cardboard box beneath Robert's bed, and they were recuperating nicely. Their appetites had returned with a vengeance, and now they were eating twice their usual amounts. In a few more days, Robert guessed they would be begging him to go back to school.

There was a knock at the front door, and Robert followed his mother to answer it.

"Why, Glenn Torkells!" she exclaimed. "I was starting to worry I'd never see you again!"

Glenn held out a plastic grocery bag. "I got you this," he said. "I wanted to say thanks for sending over that ravioli last week."

"You brought me a present?"

He shrugged. "It's just something we had in the house."

Mrs. Arthur looked inside the bag. It contained hundreds of foil packets stamped with the words DUNWICH COSMETICS. "What are these? Shampoo samples?"

"My dad gets them from work," Glenn explained. "When they make the packets wrong—if they're too full or not full enough—he gets to take home the defects."

"Oh my gosh!" Mrs. Arthur exclaimed. "Thank you, Glenn! I won't have to buy shampoo for the rest of the year!" She insisted on giving him a hug. "Now please tell me you're coming inside for dinner."

"Would that be OK?"

"Of course it's OK! You're always welcome in our house, don't you know that? I even made extra, because I had a hunch you might come by . . ."

It was the strangest thing: Robert hadn't said anything to his mother about Glenn's problems at home, and yet she seemed to know exactly what Glenn needed to hear.

Robert grabbed a clean plate from the dish rack, Mrs. Arthur set down some silverware, and soon the three of them were talking and laughing like old times. Glenn told a joke that made milk dribble out of Robert's nose, and Mrs. Arthur didn't even seem to mind.

Since it was Friday night, they decided that Glenn would sleep over. The boys arranged some pillows and sleeping bags in the living room, and Mrs. Arthur alerted them to a terrific movie on one of the cable channels. "*Night of the Critters* starts in fifteen minutes," she said. "It's probably the scariest movie I've ever seen. Giant bugs terrorize an entire city."

"It doesn't sound *that* scary," Robert yawned.

"Sounds like a comedy," Glenn said.

The boys fixed themselves ice cream sodas and a huge bowl of popcorn. Soon afterward, Pip and Squeak came sneaking down the stairs, attracted by the smell of warm butter. Robert made a space for them under his sleeping bag, and he sneaked them popcorn throughout the movie.

As the boys predicted, *Night of the Critters* wasn't scary at all, and the special effects were terrible. The giant bugs looked like they were made of rubber, and the terrorized city looked like it was constructed from cardboard boxes. But Robert and Glenn enjoyed every minute, and they applauded when an army tank shot down a giant bumblebee.

"Boy, why didn't *we* think of that?" Glenn asked.

Mrs. Arthur was sitting behind them on the sofa, reading a romance novel. "Think of what?"

"Never mind," Robert said.

The movie was halfway over when the telephone rang, and Mrs. Arthur went into the kitchen to answer it. Robert was immediately curious; their phone didn't ring very often, especially on a Friday night. He turned down the volume on the TV and overheard his mother saying, "Of course! Hello! It's nice to hear from you . . . Really? Oh, that's great! Yes, of course, December first would be fine . . ." The conversation lasted only another minute, and Robert

couldn't make sense of it.

But as soon as Mrs. Arthur hung up, she hurried into the living room. "I've got big news," she said. "You boys are going to be so excited!"

She looked happier than Robert had seen her in ages.

"Did you win the lottery?" Glenn asked.

"It's better," she said. "I've got a new job!"

Robert was shocked. "What about the hospital?"

"This is better than the hospital. The money's better, the hours are better, I even get a paid summer vacation." She raised both arms over her head in triumph. "You're looking at the new head nurse of Lovecraft Middle School!"

Creeping into Bookstores
in September 2013!

SUBSTITUTE CREATURE

Tales from Lovecraft
Middle School #4

BY CHARLES GILMAN

Don't miss the first
three titles in the

LOVECRAFT
MIDDLE SCHOOL

SERIES

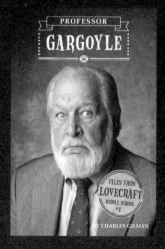
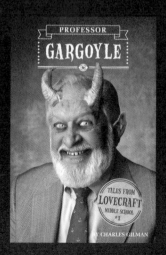

#1 PROFESSOR GARGOYLE

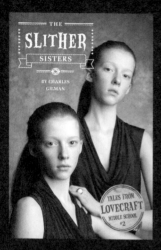 

#2 THE SLITHER SISTERS

#3 TEACHER'S PEST

HONORIS

CAUSA

AUDEAMUS

About the Author

Charles Gilman is an alias of Jason Rekulak, an editor who lives in Philadelphia with his wife, Julie, and their children Sam and Anna. When he's not dreaming up new tales of Lovecraft Middle School, he's biking along the fetid banks of the Schuylkill River, in search of two-headed rats and other horrific beasts.

About the Illustrator

From an early age, Eugene Smith dreamed of drawing monsters, mayhem, and madness. Today, he is living the dream in Chicago, where he resides with his wife, Mary, and their daughters Audrey and Vivienne.

Monstrous Thanks

To all the hard-working folks at Quirk Books, Random House Publisher Services, and National Graphics. A special tip of the antennae goes to Jonathan Pushnik, Griffin Anderson and his parents, Ed and Heidi Milano, Julie Scott, and Mary Flack.

LOVECRAFT MIDDLE SCHOOL

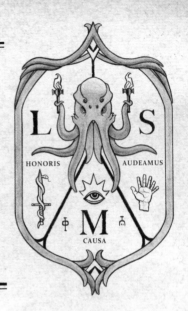

Is Now Enrolling Students Online!

- **GO** behind the scenes with author Charles Gilman!
- **READ** an interview with illustrator Eugene Smith!
- **DISCOVER** the secrets of the awesome "morphing" cover photograph!
- And much, much more!

ENROLL TODAY AT
LovecraftMiddleSchool.com